LFTFOTW

F. Richard Coldwell has worked as an art handler in many prominent New York galleries for over twenty years. *Lies From the Flies on the Wall* is his first novel.

LIES FROM THE FLIES ON THE WALL

F. RICHARD COLDWELL

HOUSTON: F
2024

Published by F
4225 Gibson Street Houston TX 77007
office@fmagazine.info

ISBN: 979-8-218-39788-3

In loving memory of Jayme Ralph

Bespoke Downs

1

IS THERE ANYTHING more vile than a bathtub with a view? I'd wager this is just the second time this fat bastard has ever even used it, the first time being the night he moved in, of course. I watch his round belly swell and relax, slowly, over and over, like a fur covered flesh island in the milky white bath water. It's really quite unsettling. To kill some time I scan the room and mentally itemize its contents: Saon free-standing soap dish, Aquanova tissue box (dark grey) with matching toilet brush holder, Lyon Beton toilet paper holder (extra small), Fonte polished chrome bathroom fixtures on a Windsor Teak vanity set, an assortment of Christian Dior perfumes and a magnificent array of Mason Pearson dark ruby bristle brushes, all lit beautifully underneath by a Collingwood walnut six-light island fixture.

"Goddammit Mr. Bernstein, don't you go drowning on me here."

I place my eight-inch serrated blade on the floor, lazily drag myself up and slide his unconscious body upward along the back of the tub, keeping his mouth and nose above water. He snorts and coughs but does not wake up. I pull his left arm from the water and grimace in embarrassment as I notice his platinum Patek Phillippe has stopped working. Pretty sloppy of me to leave it on his wrist but it's such a busy time of year, with Auction Week coming up and everything, I'm just burning out. I collapse onto the regal walnut vanity chair and pull out my phone. I have to wake him in 20 minutes for his next sales pitch so I do some Internet trolling in the meantime.

I check Twitter and #stopgagwater is trending and I can't help but smile. Five years since the merger of Larry Gagosian and Eric Prince, founder of the Blackwater Mercenary Corps, which birthed the international autocratic Fine Art and Artillery consortium known as GagWater Fine Arms LTD, the Resistance stubbornly persisted in staging meaningless but increasingly savage acts of defiance, more Fluxus than Tamil Tiger, only to have their hopes of revolution dashed upon the jagged rocks of the newest World Order. The tweets are hilarious.

@JonasMekas69_420 writes: "GW would kill u 4 kix #stopgagwater #chelseariots #poloniumfinearts"

@PenthouseArtForum writes: "Ascetic taxation and experiential oligarchies are in perfect alignment with the precepts of Thomas 1/2

2/2 Paine when he states, 'What we attain too cheaply, we esteem too lightly; it is dearness alone that gives everything its value.' #freeursfischer #stopgagwater"

Mr. Bernstein chokes and slips deeper into the water, just millimeters below the crease of his lips. I hesitate for a moment, watching to see if he stirs, but quickly go back to my phone and tweet.

"Client enthusiasm at all time high. Da new admin doomed. Suck dick @GagwaterFAL #stopgagwater #kidschoiceawards #artadvisorsusa @bespokedowns"

The tweet was a little inside joke as I used to be a GagWater employee but I'm currently working freelance. I'm presently on a job in fact, hired by a prominent NYC gallery (not GagWater) to advise Mr. Bernstein here to purchase a large secondary-market Ostrowsky, with extreme prejudice. I open my tool bag and search for phase two of my pitch. I lay the contents on the sleek marble floor. Amyl nitrate, check. Sodium thiopental, check. Seconal, Luminal, DMT, trazodone, MDMA, check. Ahh, here it is. A Narcan injection should open him up to conversation.

I had poured a cocktail of liquid MDMA and trazodone into his tea about twenty minutes ago, which was no easy task, let me tell you. It took quite a bit of time in both the planning and the actual pitch. First, I had to earn his trust, which required months of undercover work posing as his nephew, the bastard child of his estranged sister, who, after being exiled from his family home for inclinations that were natural yet forbidden, had moved to the big city with hopes of becoming a performer in an uptown cabaret. I practiced my routine in front of a mirror for endless hours until I could perform a passable version of "Meeksite" and waited for him in the lobby of his building. He was, of course, quite surprised and more than a little reluctant to make my acquaintance, but, with a little charm and a dash of "Rose's Turn," I was able to win him over. Over the succeeding weeks we met occasionally for lunch at his favorite restaurant, Uva, and I even got him to accompany me to amateur night at the legendary Café Carlyle. He was instrumental in building my confidence to audition, which I did, and for which I expect a callback any day. Fingers crossed anyway.

I jam the syringe into his shoulder, hard. His eyes bulge from his head as the Narcan takes instant effect. He should be rolling pretty hard right now, and the quick jolt of the anti-opioid has him sufficiently dazed. I run my hands along the bald spot on his head, then press his ear against my chest. He is scared but I calm him.

"It's ok, Alfred. I know. I know. Please. Shhh."

He is shaking. Maybe I went a bit heavy-handed on the pour but secondary market works are always a bitch to sell. I whisper sweetly in his ear.

"Listen buddy. Ostrowsky's use of…cave-fucking-painting…gestures are spontaneous…and necessary… graffiti… figurations and the bare …minimum…essential traits of painting as an art form. Can't you see? Alfred, he is executing the inevitable endgame of two dimensional art."

I'm tripping over my words but he is pretty high and I can feel a sale coming on.

"His market is not showing any signs of decline. After the Abu Dhabi show it will be even stronger. But this is about legacy, Alfred. Yours and Gloria's."

"Ggggaaaaa....uuuggghh...hrrmmfff..."

"Yes, that's right. Of course you'll take it. We can swap it out with the Lee Ufan in your summer home."

I place two Seconals on his tongue and massage them down his throat. Tonight is going well and honestly I don't mind sitting with him for the next couple hours, chatting and microdosing and just generally getting along. It's one of the highlights of the job and, really, it's what separates a good art advisor from a bad one. Don't get me wrong, all of our tactics could be considered ruthless, often cruel, but there is no denying that some of us have found a way to do the job with compassion. Well, if not compassion, then sympathy, or, at the very least, comedy.

When I leave, Alfred Bernstein is in his bed sleeping off the effects of his art experience. Tomorrow he will purchase *F (Jet Grill)*, 2013, from my client. I'll receive my commission and get ready for Auction Week!

2

MY NAME IS BESPOKE DOWNS. I'm an art advisor based in NYC. I deal in primary and secondary market works of contemporary art. For consultation please DM me at @ Bespokedowns4realz or fax me at (212) 555-7168 or meet me on the corner of Fulton and Throop under the awning of the fish market next Wednesday at 2:45 a.m.

This is not the sort of profession one just stumbles into. You can't just answer an ad in NYFA. It requires the same organizational trust as a Mafia family, the refined taste of a sommelier, a postgraduate degree in Art History and Curatorial Science, the skill set of a Navy Seal and the scruples of a State Corrections executioner.

I was groomed for this profession since my seventh birthday, when my adoptive father, Leo Castelli, first picked me out of a line up of fifteen preteen boys. Saint Agnes Orphanage in Parsippany, NJ, had some peculiar traditions. For one, every boy was given the same birthday, October 1. This was mostly done for budgetary reasons but it had the effect of putting together boys in the same age group that were at significantly different stages in physical development. It was on that day, every year, that they loosened their parental restrictions and allowed a boy to be adopted into a for-profit corporate conglomerate. This year, the USFAA was choosing a ward. Although Papa Leo was the face of the organization, I now count half a dozen of the nation's top gallerists and curators among my parents.

Also, we were each strongly encouraged to adopt the persona of a contemporary pop star and factor their idiosyncrasies into our own personality. It being 1985, my best friend was one of four Huey Lewises. The class bully was Sting and the bullied were usually Weird Als. You've probably guessed from the horizontal stripe of makeup across my nose, I was Adam Ant. In many ways, I still kind of am. As Mr. Castelli took me by the hand and walked me out of the orphanage, through the parking lot and into his silver BMW, I swear I heard him humming "Whip In My Valise" contentedly to himself.

I was enrolled at the Vincenzo Peruggia School of Curatorial Science and undertook the prerequisite courses for my profession almost immediately. Scientific studies have shown that childhood is the most opportune time for learning a language so my course load was as follows:

Chinese. Wu dialect. The language of the Peking Opera but with such little mutual intelligibility between varieties and sub-groups that my primary focus was an urban class Shanghainese, which allowed me access to a certain demographic of art buyer.

Russian. Specifically a Muscovite dialect which, being centralized in a transitional zone, forced me to learn hundreds of smaller scale variants of pronunciation, intonation, vocabulary and grammar. However, as it turns out, my primary contact with Russian speaking people mostly involves banking transactions. Perhaps several years of Pushkin translations weren't necessary after all. Still great though.

French. Creole. Jacamo-fin-na-ney-mother-fucker.

I wrote my middle school thesis on comparing the phonetic differences between the highly localized accents of South Philadelphia, the linguistic equivalent of sorting through trash. I took extra credit classes, just hedging my bets for the long run, and became fluent in the forbidden Afroasiatic language Oromo.

It was also important to begin my physical training at an early age, to instill good habits and muscle tone. The VPSCS was more like a military academy than a middle school: Muay Thai before school, Marine Corps Martial Arts after lunch, Krav Maga immediately after school. We were strongly encouraged to fight amongst ourselves and honestly, these were the best days of my life. I felt so alive as a child. Every moment was lived to its fullest because, at any moment, a fellow student might've snuck up behind me with piano wire and twisted it around my throat. Sure, my white bandana might dull the wire's edge, but it could've still suffocated me, or even popped my head like a baby dandelion. I never took any breath for granted. In fact, I was decidedly more aggressive than most and exhibited a ferocity that got me quickly recognized by my teachers and babysitters. I blamed it on hormones, but we all knew it was simple bloodlust.

My education in Art History did not begin in earnest until much later, when I turned eleven. At first, it was the usual undergrad bullshit curriculum. Third grade: Proto-Renaissance, Southern Baroque, Byzantine and early Medieval Art. Fourth grade: West African Art: Liberia and Sierra Leone, European and American Architecture, etc. It was so mind-numbingly dull that I often found my mind straying, childlike and pure, into daydreams so vibrant they stiffened me.

I'd often fantasize about falling in love and living with my fellow orphan and classmate little Flavor Flav. In these dreams, we had a two-story carriage house in the municipal center of Hackensack, NJ. We had a little yard surrounded by a wrought iron fence where our six dogs lived and played among six Joel Shapiro sculptures. In my utopian fantasy, I stood with Lil' Flav hand in hand, on our rickety wooden porch, proudly watching our full-grown pit bulls play and shit, wriggle and piss, roll around and fight each other, piss again, fight again, snuggle and eat grass and, at the end of every day, curl up next to their very own column of abstract garbage for a long night of snoring and doggie dreams. Together we'd watch our pups until we were sure every last one was asleep. Then we'd fry up some popcorn on the stove and plop down on the couch. Maybe he'd do a little parody and we'd giggle, or maybe I'd say something awkward and we'd blush, but inevitably we'd end up with our VR headsets on, each engaged in separate war fantasies, equally violent and impressively realistic. Every day the same daydream. Every day the same misadventure.

It wasn't until junior high that I really got excited about the art market. It was then that I became enamored with the combination of art historical scholarship, business acumen, and psychological warfare unique to today's art exchange. If it wasn't for a few dedicated and demanding teachers, I may have strayed into an altogether different profession, perhaps taxidermy, or I may have become an MTA employee. But, under the strict tutelage of such renowned professors as William Acquavella, Charles Egan and Andre Emmerich, my passion for a career in the art world was turned into an obsession. They taught me the importance of focus. They taught me that through sheer force of will I could really make a difference. They instilled in me a respect for history, a masterful understanding of the tendencies and nuances of the art market, a desire to push boundaries, and to not be afraid of making mistakes, which I never did.

Of all of the teachers I was honored to study under, it is to Professor Boone I owe the biggest debt of gratitude. It is to her I owe my sense of exquisite savagery. She is responsible for my manhood in every understanding of the word. I loved her so intensely that I yearned for her approval and I was desperate for her attention. In class, I was ferocious, but that was not enough. In martial arts, I was studious and cruel, but she still denied me her affection. I smashed a Duchamp sculpture at the PMA and she acted as if she didn't care. Until one morning, very early, on the south lawn of the Isabella Stewart Gardner Museum, with a Rembrandt painting tucked under my arm, our relationship was eternally consummated. The details of our encounter must remain secret, but the simple fact that only she and I survive to know the glorious details of that spring morning is enough for me. I like to think that occasionally she reflects on that day, its ruthlessness and our promises made, her stomach tightening with affection like mine does.

I graduated Summa Cum (lol) Laude and immediately hopped on a plane to Central America, where I filled the next decade (plus) with a cultural lewdness and indiscriminate appreciation for all things compositionally satisfying. Really, I was just indulging the attributes that have come to define men of my particularly randy age. I dabbled in painting and built up a sizable body count. I wrote conceptual manifestos and found my way onto Interpol watchlists. I may even have become a father, a padre, an otet, or a pe´re. After I had my fill of museum hopping and espionage, I made my way back to the city in a caravan of refugees and took a job as an associate salesperson at GagWater. I killed an intern on the very first day. From that point forward, I was respected and treated, much to my delight, as a threat.

3

I KNEW MY FIRST SALE would have to be a big one, and it was. Cy Twombly, *Min-Oe*, 1951. Oil on canvas. Sold for $70 mil to the one and only David Koch.

Gaining access to one of the richest men in the world is not easy. I had to approach my sales pitch from multiple fronts, but I had done my research. I was keenly aware of his partiality to pre-Raphaelite poetry and his fondness for the heroes of the American Outlaw West. The layers of security that surrounded him left me shook and intimidated. I watched his apartment. His doorman was ex-CIA. His USPS was FSB. His PCP ex-NYPD. His maid DGSE. This wouldn't be easy, but selling art rarely is. It would require a stroke of luck, which came in the form of an uncommonly slutty receptionist at Mr. Koch's dentist's office. Her loose lips and slick pillow talk gave me the *in* I needed, and so I hatched my plan.

My strategy would require a disguise. I was quite fond of a plumber persona I used during grad school, and I was eager to dust off that sexy jumpsuit. I've always had a disdain for blue-collar professions, but I held my nose and studied up on the plebeian tradecraft. You see, my plumber disguise comes with an incredible backstory that I just couldn't resist. As the story goes, the plumber's father, believe it or not, fled Germany after the Allied victory to avoid prosecution for crimes against humanity. He settled in Zacatecas, Mexico, took a wife and had a son. He traded in his Nazi instruments of torture for a toolbox and a white van and made a respectable living with what little indoor plumbing existed in the village. In lieu of paying protection money, he offered the services of his son to the local cartel, and soon his boy climbed the ranks and began running contraband by sea to Cuba. It was on one of these transports that the son first caught the eye of the niece of Joaquín Guzmán, who had stowed away on the vessel. Together they set off on an inflatable raft for the Florida Keys. After three years of misadventure on an alligator farm in the Everglades, they took a Peter Pan bus to Port Authority. Once they'd settled into an apartment in New Rochelle, the son managed to obtain a spot in the UA Local Union No. 1, and found himself working endless hours at his father's trade, as a plumber in and around the city. Sure, it took a toll on his marriage, but with the birth of their second child came a million more reasons to take every opportunity for overtime. They found themselves in a vicious cycle, but still, their love endured.

That day, he found himself in the bowels of a penthouse at 7** Park Ave, tapping into the main water supply line. He had fashioned a five-gallon rubber bladder filled with concentrated, saccharin-based simple syrup and cut with just a pinch of methamphetamine, which he was able to stow between the studs in the wall. He routed a feeder line to the water supply, being sure to bypass any in-house filtration system.

The immigrant plumber then, much to the chagrin of his wife and kids, was forced to take an indefinite sabbatical. To him I am grateful, and I will surely need to step into his life again someday. The plumber ruse represented only one early facet of this particular sales pitch, of course. The second wave involved infiltrating Mr. Koch's dentist, and some truly nasty business.

After sleeping with the dentist's receptionist, I was able to discover that the dentist had developed an affinity for the ole Captain Cody, the Fluff, OC, the Dillies, the 512's or as you probably know it, Hillbilly Heroin. By picking his pocket once a week for four weeks straight (not so easy!) I was able to swap out his biscuits with a significantly higher dosage, thus insuring his pliability when the time came.

Perhaps more importantly, I think, was the fact that, on the night I took his receptionist up the fudge tunnel, I managed to note her brand of perfume (a very nice Frédéric Malle floral) and also take a multitude of highly indecent photos, many of them involving dental roleplay. For weeks, I hunted the poor dentist, causing him to be delayed from work every evening with increasingly unlikely excuses. Of course I caused traffic jams, but I also set fires, left large animal carcasses on or around his car, flattened his tires and tossed objects (hand weights, bowling balls, icon statues, a very expensive Chateau Vitus) onto his windshield. To cap it off, I waited for him every day in various disguises, and blasted him with a cloud of his receptionists' Carnal Flower. Surely his wife, the true love of his life, was quickly growing tired of his excuses, his apparent infidelity, and his increasingly unstable drug addiction. I know I was. It was only a matter of time until the phone in his office rang, and his flexible receptionist took an appointment for Mr. Koch, whose cavities seemed to be flaring up, thanks to the amphetamine-laced sugar water pumping through the penthouse faucets.

That call did arrive, exactly eight weeks since the beginning of my first-ever sales pitch. It seems Mr. Koch's incisors and bicuspids were beginning to rapidly erode due to accumulated bacteria and hypo-salivation, and he was in need of emergency dental care. I was so excited. Finally after all those years of study, of hard work and unflinching ferocity, I was getting my opportunity for a sale. I had had an outfit picked out for this occasion for years, but the moment it was actually *real*, I couldn't make up my mind. In all of my fantasies of this day I wore a Tom Ford O'Connor base sharkskin two-piece suit (bright navy) with a pink neck bandana and Air Jordan 4's, along with the customary stripe of makeup across my nose and a feather or two in my hair. But when the time came I wanted to wear something, I don't know, *showier*. I decided on a Gucci embroidered fur jacket (white, goat/mink/lamb fur, women's M) with a spread collar and straight hem, matched with a pair of Dolce and Gabbana tapered slacks and classic Air Jordan 1's. I tried multiple looks with my white bandana and eventually settled on a wristband, with my usual syringe of sodium thiopental tucked in discreetly for later. Looking this good made me feel confident, perhaps over confident.

The evening before the appointment, I texted Mrs. Dentist a blurry photo or two of some of that nasty business I got into with the receptionist. Under close inspection, say in a court of law, it could be proven that the man involved in the scene was not the dentist himself, but I really didn't give a shit. The object of this whole exercise was to throw his house into chaos, which I thoroughly enjoyed watching, dressed as a homeless man, from the sidewalk outside their apartment. I also texted the pics to the receptionist's family members. All of them. I'm not sure why.

In retrospect, it proved wholly unnecessary to torment the dentist and his spouse. I think I was taking out some frustration at the fact that I was unable to have access to the actual target of the sale, due to his high profile nature, and was therefore denied one of the more enjoyable aspects of a sales pitch. Regardless, I believe in not second-guessing one's successes.

Needless to say, on the day of the appointment, the receptionist did not show up. There was enough disorder in the office that no one suspected anything when I claimed to have an appointment. My outfit caused some sideways glances, but I had been clever enough to remove one of my lateral incisors prior to the appointment, so any doubts about the legitimacy of my presence were assuaged with a smile. Mr. Koch was quickly ushered through the waiting room and into the office. He was accompanied by a security goon in an off the rack black suit (for protection against pushy art salesmen, no doubt) who took a seat in the waiting room and flipped through an issue of Sports Illustrated, the February issue with a long-form exposé of the absolutely hilarious men's Spanish Paralympics basketball controversy.

I waited until the goon was completely transfixed by the article to make my move. I pepper sprayed the bastard then quickly pounced upon him with a roll of plastic stretch wrap I had hidden in my Louis Vuitton handbag. I had him securely bound to the chair in no time. The other patients got the picture pretty quickly and were out the door. I kicked down the door to the dentist's office and with both arms outstretched, I cocked my revolvers and said, "Two souls but with a single thought! Two hearts that beat as one!"

I smashed the dentist in the mouth with the handle of my revolver and he collapsed like a wet rag. I pointed both barrels directly at my client, who looked great even with the paper bib hanging from his neck, and said, "The poetry of the Earth is never dead."

I straddled him.

"A thing of beauty is a joy forever. Do you know what I mean, David?"

He was terrified, but sharp as a tack.

"Keats," he said.

I knew then that I'd be making this sale.

I placed the oxygen mask over his face and recited all fourteen lines of "When I Have Fears." We were reduced to tears before the final stanza. My revolvers bounced up and down on his belly as he sobbed and I sobbed. It was beautiful. I slowly slipped my arm around his neck and was able to just barely twist open the regulator of the oxygen tank. Hyperoxia was kicking in but I was careful not to cause too much oxidental damage to his wealthy cell membranes, lest

his retinas detach from his eyes and no Twombly he buys.
His sobs turned to whimpers then stopped altogether. I
removed the mask from his face, taking thick strings of saliva with it. His chin collapsed to his chest, and he was deep
asleep. For a moment I thought about canceling the viewing
I had planned, so confident was I that the sale was made,
but I was just so excited and had worked so hard and was
perhaps a bit overeager.

It was great. Mr. Koch came to in a large vacant stretch of
broken blacktop underneath the Whitestone Bridge, on the
Bronx side, sitting on an overstuffed, brown, cracked leather
recliner (fully reclined).

Parked roughly thirty feet in front of him were three
extra-large shipping containers. I had set up a few burn barrels around the lot for dramatic effect. Please note: I had
not subjected my client to any chemical stimuli for this final
stretch of my pitch. We had made too strong of a connection, I was naïve enough to believe, for me to deny him the
sober opportunity to fall in love with the childlike yet aus-
tere masterpiece I was about to present to him.

Crouching on my knees and out of his immediate line of
sight, I rubbed my knuckles together nervously. I could feel
the spiritual presence of a legacy of fine art sales virtuosos
crouching right behind me. I could smell the sulfur waft-
ing from the ghosts of Seth Seiglaub, Nigel Greenwood,
Ambroise Vollard, groovy Bob Fraser and other notable
crackerjacks. I took a long, deep breath then leapt to my
feet. It was immediately clear to me that my outfit was perfect. I presented myself to him in an almost solemn way.

"I'm so glad you came, David. Honestly, when I first
heard whispers that you may be interested in this painting,
I dismissed them outright. I didn't think, and I apologize
for my bluntness, that its poetic abstemiousness would res-
onate with a man of your worldly acridity, or that you would
appreciate the ultimate sense of irony. But when we met, at

the office, I was floored by the depth of your sympathies. I knew then that you were the born owner, destined to live and love and suffer and laugh alongside this sophisticatedly difficult example of Post War art."

I could tell I was nervous, but could he?

"David, behind me you see three viewing rooms. I'm not going to lie, in two of them you'd find something quite horrible. I mean really fucking bad, David, like Paul McCarthy with a chainsaw bad, and I don't want anything to happen to you. So I need you to pick the good one. The one with *your* Twombly, David. Take all the time you need but please, not too long. I dare say my day has been as difficult, if not more so, than yours, and I'd like to keep this moving."

I stood for as long as I could. It frustrated me that, instead of settling into a deep contemplation of the work, instead of trying to hone in on a psychic connection to extrapolate which shipping container/viewing room would save his life, he was simply confused. I had too much respect for the man to let him get pathetic, so I intervened and yanked him from the recliner and onto the concrete. He screamed in excitement. I didn't mean to drag him but I did. I dropped him about 10 feet in front of the containers. He looked tired. I unwrapped my bandana from my wrist, tossed it to him and said, "Death is the true yea-sayer, Dave. It stands before eternity and says only: Yes.'"

David started crying inexcusably loud. Fortunately, I had a machete. Pulling it dramatically from beneath my fur coat, I pointed it to the sky and said, "No great art has ever been made without the artist knowing danger. Hello? Anything? Rrrrraaaiiiinnnneeerrrr....?" Admittedly, I was getting frustrated. "Choose a fucking door, my man!"

David fell forward with a thud, in the direction of viewing room number two. He was really starting to bum me out. I walked over to the tool kit I had stashed behind a burn barrel. I dug out a vial of cocaine and my works. I was afraid

David might be mad at me for shooting him up and denying him the pure experience I knew he wanted, but he was useless to me asleep. I sat cross-legged next to him and held a flame to my spoon. The syringe pulled the coke through the cotton swab, and I gently slid it into his vein. In a matter of seconds he breathed deeply and inhaled. He looked blissful. I was so proud.

"My god, it's you," he said.

"Yes. It's me, Bespoke Downs. Be-spoke Dow-ns. And it's time. Do you remember which door you chose?"

He was so high, but at least he was paying attention. He seemed truly present for the first time all night. I spun around in a grand gesture and pointed to the middle shipping container.

"You chose number two! Let's see what's inside!"

I thrust the long vertical security locks downward and swung the doors open. The interior of the industrial steel box was immaculate if not a bit ostentatious. Glossy hardwood floors shone underneath Eurofase lighting tracks. The walls were a perfectly flat Decorators' White. Installed in the middle wall of the room, at a perfect eye-catching center height of 59 inches, was the artwork: Cy Twombly's *Min-Oe*, 1951.

Then came the moment when David Koch earned my eternal admiration. It took all of his strength to pull himself up from the spotless hardwood floor, but he did it. His skin was cadaverous yet wet with perspiration. Very gross. His shirt collar was soiled and his slacks wrinkled. But I swear, the way he reached so deeply into his spirit, the way he pulled one last ounce of determination from the depth of his wretched soul and feebly pushed himself onto his knees, and then his feet, struck me very profoundly. He swayed like a young tree for a moment and then gathered himself. My emotions overwhelmed me and I instinctively clenched my fists. It's always been a quirk of mine to hit someone when moved emotionally, but I restrained myself. The purity of his hatred for me was practically holy.

I handed him his cell phone. He took it and walked in front of the artwork, took a moment to gather himself, then made a call.

"It's me, yes. I'm going to need you to make a wire transfer. Details forthcoming. What? Indeed. I've never been better, actually."

4

WITHIN A FEW DAYS everyone at GagWater knew my name. I started showing up at 11:00 and leaving by 4:00. I wore cologne but no deodorant. I commanded respect and it was offered freely. I quickly became one of LG's top salespeople and excelled at my craft for ten very profitable years. I was feared throughout the art world, until one day, when it all came crashing to a halt.

I was alone in the elevator at 980 Madison, going down. I had my headphones on, volume loud, and was singularly focused on this Big L jam when, apparently, the Resistance crashed a Sprinter van right through the glass façade into the lobby, where it skidded to a halt right between two massive Ed Ruscha paintings. All I could hear was that sweet 808 from my Beats By Dre, but when the elevator doors slid open I was confronted with absolute chaos.

There were at least five Resistance members scurrying around the lobby engaged in various *artistic actions*. It was hard to focus on just one to truly ingest its meaning but I made a point to try. After all, the Resistance is awesome. Always dressed in the most stylish and tasteful threads, always current season. Shit like Rick Owens, Off-White, Ann Demeulemeester, with a little flash of (vintage) Vivienne Westwood every now and then. They wore masks of course. Bandanas, ski masks with skull designs, animal faces, potato sacks, shit like that. They hardly oozed wealth but they looked like a million bucks.

To my immediate left, a young gentleman in a button-up Tacklo Mary jacket, APC New Cure jeans, and one of those transparent plastic Halloween masks with painted on lips and eyebrows, was unsheathing a large hunting knife. He turned to his right and cut a six-foot square from the center of Ruscha's *The End*, 1991. He ripped the square from the stretcher, made an eight-inch slit in its center and slid it over his head as a poncho. It was pretty funny and kind of reminded me of an old Jannis Kounellis performance but when I saw that he cut an additional hole through which to poke his erection, I couldn't help but flash him a big thumbs up.

Standing on top of the Sprinter van was a rail-thin man in his forties wearing a sharp pair of blue Alexander McQueen cropped trousers with tuxedo stripes, a Saint Laurent patchwork puffer vest with a matching patchwork balaclava. He had a bullhorn slung around his neck, and held an open can of cyanocarbon in one hand, which sent a steady stream of thick, white smoke bouncing off of the ceiling, and a sign in his other which read, "Original Manuscript of Steele Dossier Breaks Auction Records!" The lobby was a holy mess. Three other voguish Resisters were lighting a bonfire on what used to be *Home With Complete Electronic Security System*, 1982. A few civilians remained inside, either trapped beneath rubble or frozen in fear. I could hear Herbie Hancock's "Sextant" blaring out from the Sprinter van, right in the middle of Bernie Maupin's kazoo solo. Then something caught my eye. There was a scene developing up near the security desk that demanded my attention.

A young woman, perfect in every way, had a hatchet pressed to a security guard's neck. From a distance her profile looked like a Matisse cut-out, her contours part tundra wolf, part comic book heroine. The blood splatters on her Rag and Bone floral blouse dripped down her Helmut Lang straight leather mini skirt, snaked down her slender legs in a flirtatious spiral, and landed onto her Golden Goose Superstars.

A cardboard bank robber mask obscured her eyes but I could still see they were an unholy, inky black. It was her large, fur, Cossack Papakha that really had me excited though.

I stepped out of the elevator pulling my bandana over my mouth and nose but never once taking my eyes off the scene by the security station. I stepped over glass and rubble and past the bonfire *motif in light*. Then, for no apparent reason, the woman turned her attention directly on me. She flashed me a hostile glare like that Afghani babe from that classic *National Geographic* cover. She pulled the security guard into a headlock, keeping the jagged blade of the hatchet pressed against his carotid artery, and advanced in my direction.

Her eyes never left mine.

I stopped in my tracks as she approached. When she was close enough to speak amidst the noise and tumult of the slick uptown lobby, I was taken aback. At first, I thought the horrible stench of B.O. was coming from the security dude, but no, there was something distinctly feminine about it. Nevertheless, it was quite rank. It was an unexpected character trait and it made me curious as to what other surprises she had in store.

She choked the guard even tighter and forced his chin upward, so that he and I were forced into eye contact. He was terrified, as was I, for him. Then she spoke, slowly and with purpose.

"Draw a straight line and follow it."

I was floored. I knew immediately what to say but I had to hold back, lest I vomit all over the poor guard due to the increasing noxiousness of this horrible angel's armpits. She began to walk away, dragging the man along with her. When I felt my stomach settle enough to speak, I took my chance.

"Hey. *Composition 1960? #10, to Bob Morris?*"

She turned her head momentarily to smile at me over her shoulder, and as she did, she dragged the edge of the hatchet across the man's throat, cleanly cutting his windpipe and arteries back to the spine. She proceeded to drag his lifeless body behind her as she walked out the front doors, leaving a straight line of blood smeared across the polished granite floor.

I stood silent and lovestruck. I took a step, then another directly in front of that one, like a tightrope walk through the anarchy, and kept walking that way down the avenue, through the crowds and police, across 77th Street, and through the park, eventually falling asleep beneath the Bethesda Fountain. That was three months ago today.

I tendered my resignation the following afternoon.

5

I KEEP AN EYE on all Resistance social media. I frequent the clubs they are rumored to turn up at. I bought a police scanner that actually comes in so useful it's become part of my normal routine. I've met a few Resistance Grrls and they were all great in bed, but only she makes my heart pinch. Never really thought of myself as sentimental but here I am, all gaga and puppy love.

The commission check for the Ostrowsky sale to Mr. Bernstein just came in and I'm thinking about taking a little break. Although I'm disgustingly successful, no one has ever accused me of being a workaholic. I was considering a holiday on the Amalfi Coast, surrounded by the lemon scented coastal air, but I don't want to go into Auction Week without a plan. There's much research to do, both on current market trends and also the phobias and neurosis of potential buyers. I have flight manifests to go through, hotel reservations to hack, false identities to actualize, galleries to break into, auction houses to case...

It gets so overwhelming if you look at it all at once. I find it much more manageable when I personalize my work. I need to focus on identifying a client. Once I have a face to put to the sale it becomes a true labor of love. All of the tediousness of the planning is no longer a chore. It is my straight line and I follow it to the end. Delivering a truly great sales pitch is the only time I feel connected to people. Maybe it's the thrill of the chase but it feels more like passion. When I research my clients I step into their metaphorical skin and try to diagnose what ails them. If I can identify an abnormality I can spin that into a sale. I become the opposite of a doctor, an anti-doctor, seeking only to exacerbate their hysteria.

The goal is never to completely stupefy a client but to just tinker around a bit with their maladjustments. Obviously, making a vegetable out of your client isn't going to do anyone any good, which has happened to less talented sales people I should add. But if you can tenderize their psyche like a steak, you will find them to be significantly more agreeable to your pitch.

We aren't barbarians of course. No respectable fine art dealer would place an important work of art with a client who wouldn't foster a lofty appreciation for it. In fact, if it wasn't for the elevated commitment to adhering to this principle, I believe the market itself would cease to flourish. Without it we would be little more than criminals. Nietzsche once said that "ultimately it is desire, not the desired, that we love." But I believe what he meant to say is, "Get out there and sell the sizzle."

I check Twitter.

@RobertaSmiffnWesson says: "Da riots n amstrdm have had surprisng perk 2 #auctionweek"

@PissChrist58008 says: "Terror on the Jitney! Carnage on Hamptons bound orgy bus #auctionweek #terroronjitney"

For a second I consider that this gesture on the Hamptons Jitney was performed by the grrl I've been searching for, but it didn't have any of her distinguishing characteristics. Although I find myself impressed by the elegance of the performance, it just didn't meet her established criteria. First, this Jitney attack could not be reasonably interpreted as the enactment of a La Monte Young performance score, as I believe all of hers can. I also believe that she has been intentionally repeating La Monte Young performance scores solely for my benefit. She wants me to find her. And so far, I have been woefully inadequate.

Following the ruckus in the GagWater lobby, there was another Resistance gesture that caught my attention and alerted me to her intentions. At a cocktail party at Glenn Lowry's midtown digs, a beautiful Re*sister* had disguised herself as a National Medal of Honor Award-winning piano player and managed to push a Steinway Model D Concert Grand through a smooth, white plaster wall, unfortunately taking the panicked but strangely ebullient Marina Abromović with it, in an actualization of *Piano Piece for Terry Riley #1, 1960*. When the performance was over, she elbowed through the stunned crowd of bluebloods and leaped onto the windowsill (not easy to do in 11 cm Jimmy Choo white crystal sandals) and released a jar of East Asian weaver ants into the room. I obviously understood this last part as a beacon to me, a nod to my Adam Ant inspired garb. I was just thrilled to know that she was thinking of me the way I was of her.

I scoured the events listings online to see if any public event could be a poetic target for a La Monte Young score. It turns out, however, that it wasn't the setting of her next gesture that made it poetic, but the strict adherence to the exact wording of its author. When La Monte Young wrote the score for *Composition #3, 1960* the instructions were as follows:

> *Announce to the audience when the performance will begin and end. Then announce that they are free to do whatever they want during the performance.*

So when she trapped the viewers at the opening reception for the Louise Nevelson exhibition at Lockheed-Pace Gallery behind a ten-foot wall of fire (with a wink to the score of *Composition #2, Build a Fire, 1960*) and announced the performance would be considered over when they were all dead, she went on to announce that they were, indeed, free to do whatever they wished for the duration of the performance. And when they pulled the painted black wood structures from the gallery walls and threw together a makeshift bridge through the fire, she was hardly in a position to intervene. There was a transcendent frenzy as the hip gallery crowd climbed over one another across the large burnt oak assemblages to the safety of the Chelsea sidewalk.

I was surprised to see her settle for a body count of zero, but also a bit proud of her puritanical adherence to the artist's instructions. Kudos. I feared, however, that this moment of restraint, along with an obvious frustration at my ineptitude, would cause her to overcompensate. Her next performance would be a massacre.

I'm absolutely horrified to think how pitiful I must have looked to her. There are only six days left before the start of Auction Week, plenty of time for her to plan a magnificent performance but hardly enough time for me to tend to my responsibilities. In my defense, I have quite a few pressing matters to attend to at the moment. I'm trying to take my young solo career very seriously. I barely get any sleep.

For instance, Wednesday morning I found myself deep in Queens, abducting a livery driver and driving his car to JFK to pick up Mr. Jun Wei, a Chinese cybersecurity analyst and contemporary art collector. I knew Mr. Wei would not change drivers once he arrived so it was imperative I was his first contact. I'd likely have the opportunity to eavesdrop, especially if I was able to conceal my fluency in Mandarin. I spotted him gathering his luggage and put myself in position to be seen without alerting him to my eagerness.

He didn't have any security with him, but he was dangerous in many ways. I'd have to play this angle with a light hand. Surely he or his team would sweep for bugs, intercept my text messages and monitor my online browsing, but this particular aspect of my pitch didn't require any deep infiltration to still be beneficial. I can infer quite a bit simply from the knowledge of his whereabouts, his hotel, his appointments, his chance encounters. It does, however, come with very challenging demands on my schedule. The majority of my days are now spent reclining in the driver seat of an Audi A8 waiting on Mr. Wei, flipping through stacks of printed out research I prepared the previous evening. In them are laser printed papers of venue research, annotated provenance, art law and its particular relevance to certain dealers, collectors and other stakeholders. All last night was spent downloading and printing the latest market analysis to identify a trend my client may be able to capitalize on. I study the auction lots and bibliographies. It's tedious and borderline prehistoric. I know they'll be expecting me to browse on my phone so I use the opportunity to scour the weekly event listings in search of a potential target for a particularly savage Fluxus gesture.

There are listings for church events, book signings, council forums, you name it. Nothing jumps out at me as being particularly attractive to her. I check what openings would be happening this week and there are quite a few that could be an enticing location for a violent tableau but they hardly fit the La Monte Young parameters. Chris Ofili at Zwirner/Shkreli, Frank Stella at Kushner-Nahmad, Nick Cave at YeezyShainman Gallery and Walton Ford at GagWater. If I can find the time I'll try to cruise by but it's unlikely given the demands of my pitch for Mr. Wei.

6

IT IS MONDAY morning and the first VIP event of Auction Week is Wednesday. I'm sitting outside the Carlyle Hotel waiting for my client and his entourage. My research papers are safely hidden away in a custom compartment. I'm not without my doubts in regards to my plan. I'm fully committed to this 'driver' persona, and it's weak. The unfortunate livery driver who unwittingly supplied my current identity should have woken up hog-tied and naked in the courtyard of the Isaacs Houses in Yorktown by now, with an unfortunate case of short term amnesia. He seems like a great guy and I wish him the best, but there is much I still don't know about him. For instance, I'd assumed him to be right handed by the way he swung a punch at me during the abduction, but it is possible he is ambidextrous. I saw cat hair on his blazer but no wedding ring so he likely lives with his mother. His car is impeccable, leading me to believe he is quite good at his job, and I am determined to not let him down.

Mr. Wei exits the revolving doors of the hotel accompanied by two security personnel holding briefcases in their left hands. This in itself is enough to snap me to attention but combined with the fact that Mr. Wei himself is holding two black Mancini Italian leather attaché cases, one in each hand, suggests that something big is getting started. I open the rear passenger side door for him then close it. The goons get into a black Range Rover Holland and Holland that is parked behind me. I receive my next directions via text message from an unknown number. This has never happened before and it is quite unsettling. I must be vigilant.

The message instructs me to go to 1334 York Ave, Sotheby's, and park by the service entrance on 77th Street. I do as instructed. Something is going down and I fear I am woefully unprepared. I have to get a listening device on my client but surely he will be scanned once inside the building. Sotheby's has always been renowned for its barbarism, but it wasn't until after its sale to Patrick Drahi (who ultimately flipped it to Dmitry Rybolovlev) that it truly became a secondary market gulag. Following the Bouvier Affair, Mr. Rybolovlev became determined to never again fall victim to the rampant fraud in the world of fine art investing. I find both his brutality and his commitment to *amour propre* to be infinitely admirable.

I pull the Audi over on 77th Street and open the door for my client. He is quickly flanked by his security detail. Then, to my surprise, he is stopped by Sotheby's security (ex-GRU thugs no doubt) before they reach the twin doors of the service entrance. Mr. Wei and his entourage hand over the briefcases on the spot. My client is then, quite rudely, told to raise his arms while they scan him with handheld wireless signal detectors. This is my chance. They are being sloppy and I have to capitalize.

As subtly as I can manage, I pull out the three-piece portable blowgun I have hidden beneath the steering column. I wrap my microdigital sound recorder in a glob of museum wax and jam it into the blowgun, then slip behind the Audi and crouch out of site. As Mr. Wei is given the all clear and waved past security, I make my move.

I must say that holding the blowgun made of dried river cane reeds really took me back to the summer internship I completed at the United Keetoowah Federal Programs office in Oklahoma. It was there, during that humid July all those years ago, I had my first crush ever, on a shy and beautiful Cherokee girl. She taught me how to say curse words with smoke signals and, every now and then, in the aftermath of a particularly fiery sales pitch, I'll send filthy messages to her in the smoke from the burning rubble. But it was her grandmother who taught me how to shoot a blow dart with deadly accuracy.

With one deep breath I shoot the surveillance bug through the air and directly onto the lapel of Mr. Wei's Ascot Chang suit. I know it won't go undetected for long but it is worth the risk. This particular surveillance bug is set to record to a hard drive I have set up at my loft on Front Street so I'm unable to monitor it live. All for the best though, as it is imperative I maintain my alibi.

It had been confirmed they were indeed keeping an eye on my phone so I begin to browse around online, you know, staying inconspicuous. I absentmindedly flip through the results of the NBA playoffs and see the league is still being dominated by the three-point shooting of Ben Simmons. I check the *Daily News*, Page Six. The Jayden Smith armed standoff is going into its third day. I avoid Twitter. Normally I would have made my alias a Twitter account for an occasion such as this, but I was so distracted by tracking the Resistance's movements that I never got around to it. I know my alias won't hold for long after the discovery of the bug, and I have much to do in very little time. At best, I figure, I'll have until tonight, when Mr. Wei hands his suit to the dry cleaners for the evening.

I'm searching the Time Out NY app for event listings when something catches my eye. The 10th Annual Lepidopterology Convention is being held this evening in the Rainbow Room of Rockefeller Center. It is advertised that London Applied Entomology will be exhibiting a newly discovered example of *Anartia Fatima*, the beautiful Branded Peacock butterfly. This could be the setting for the gesture I was waiting for.

La Monte Young's *Composition 1960 #5*:
Turn a butterfly loose in a performance area.
The performance may be considered over when the butterfly flies
out of the room.

I can feel in my bones that she would choose this venue
for this performance score. It is no coincidence that Rockefeller Center is also the home of Christie's Auction House.
I take a minute to consider how she may interpret these
instructions, and all of my imaginings are quite bloody. I
also understand that this may be my last chance to reach her,
to show her I understand her art and that I want to be a part
of it. To collaborate through body and soul like a modern
day Andre and Mendieta. I will not let her down again.

The Entomologists dinner is scheduled for 7 p.m., immediately followed by the presentation of the rare butterfly. I
begin to think of ways to shake myself free of Mr. Wei when
the decision is made for me. A bullet shatters the passenger
side window, very nearly taking off my nose. I duck my head,
throw the gear shift into drive, floor it, and turn to see my
client's two security goons running behind, guns blazing.
Glass shatters around me and little pops of impact appear
on the dashboard.

I turn right onto FDR Drive but am forced to abandon
the Audi when I T-bone a taxi. I leap over car hoods and
then the large, stone highway dividers to get into the city.
I eventually find myself spinning on the corner of 55th and
First Ave. I zigzag my way to the nearest subway and head
downtown. It takes over an hour to get to my loft because I
take evasive measures to be sure I am not followed.

When I get to my loft I know right away that something
else is very wrong. Propped in my foyer, right in front of my
Vera floor mirror (with jewelry armoire) is Damien Hirst's
stunning if not gratuitously oversized *I am Become Death,
Shatterer of Worlds,* 2005, which I do not own. Around me

are hundreds of pigeons, many of them dead, filling the entrance hall. Underneath the large, rhythmically vibrant macrolepidopteran artwork lies the crushed carcass of a large Manchurian crane, in its mouth a sealed envelope. I take my time pulling the envelope from its sleek, olive colored beak. The majestic bird is dissected perfectly in half, Black Dahlia style, save for its long neck, which hangs by a tendon from its left shoulder. Its wings are spread symmetrically across the floor. Warm blood still burbles beneath the high-gloss black lacquer frame, and bright red streams of blood flow across the bird's swollen chest like lava down a fucking snow pile. My god, is she still here?

I hear a crash, then another, in the eastern exposure of the renovated textile factory I inherited from Chuck Close (long story). A quick five seconds later and I'm standing in my office, windows smashed, desk flipped over, files and records molested. I hear a voice. A man speaking slowly with a Chinese accent. The receiver unit from the surveillance bug I planted on my client is playing the recording I made today. Surely she would have stolen it had it not been bolted to the floor. I consider chasing her but don't really want to hasten the inevitable end to our game. In my hand I hold the envelope from the crane's mouth. On it are simply the words *October 1960*. I tear into it but it's empty, save for the smashed remains of a single stink ant.

If I had known that Auction Week was going to be so hectic, I never would have bothered pitching that Ostrowsky to Mr. Bernstein. I know it will exhaust me, but I roll a joint, grab a bottle of Robitussin and lie down in the disheveled office to dream the next few hours away. It is the only way I can stomach listening to the secret recording of Mr. Wei's tedious afternoon. I slow it down to 1/4 speed, light the joint and sip some syzzurp.

7

IF YOU'RE NOT freshly baked, take a minute to get right, then check out these highlights:

12:36 p.m. Elevator of Sotheby's Auction House. Near the 8th floor. A conversation in Mandarin, roughly translating to as follows: *Damn son, check dat ass. For real yo. All these American bitches are just so thicc. Love dat fat ass cuz.*

12:38 p.m. Elevator of Sotheby's Auction House. 14th floor. The sound of shuffling as people leave and enter the elevator. Then a cloaked conversation. Os exis: *Mr. Wei, I am a friend of Mr. de Pury*. The man continues, *We like the new agriculture, in Holland. Do you like it? The new agriculture in Holland?* Some mumbled conversation in Mandarin follows. My client clears his throat. The elevated tone to his next words betray his professionalism. *I do like it. I like it very much.*

12:42 p.m. Reception desk on high-security Private Client floor. The sounds of party horns and kazoos. There is the unmistakable pop of a spring-loaded superfine classic multicolored glitter bomb. The sound of cheering. Mr. Wei is confused, *What the fuck?* The distinct high voice of Ms. Jasmin Colmes, newly hired receptionist on the 23rd floor says, *Oh my god! You're number 1K! Our thousandth client! We are just so happy to see you today, Mr.… Get the fuck out of my face, bitch. Please, sir. We have a TV crew here to interview our very special client. Come this way, please. Slut, I'll cut your throat.* There is a brief scuffle, a crunching sound, followed by silence. Briefly thereafter my client's security goons burst from the service entrance doors and pumped bullets into my once gorgeous Audi sedan.

Maybe it is the Kush or maybe it is the Tussin, but I start thinking to myself just how wonderfully diverse the agricultural exports of the Netherlands are. Such fertile soil, top quality produce and well processed dairy, all exported with an ancient knack for trading. It is a testament to the *esprit des corps* of the Dutch people that they maintain such high standards through countless generations.

I hop in the shower to try and wake up a bit. My pitch has gone horribly off track and I gotta try and focus. But how many times in a man's life does he get confronted with the girl of their dreams, get lured into a flirtatious avocation, and challenged to join her in a bloody expression of core artistic values? Not many, and I wasn't going to let this one slip by. Time is not my friend. I found a grey hair at the office the other day. It wasn't mine, but still.

In the shower I wank to my old school bus driver, Ms. Lewanne, as always, but immediately afterward I think of the cold-blooded temptress of the Resistance. How far did she run from my loft until she noticed I wasn't chasing her? Was she home now? In the shower? Did she correctly interpret the audio recording of Mr. Wei? She obviously knew the name de Pury, the most famous sniper during the Auction Wars, but did she decipher the part about the Robert Rauschenberg *Combine* painting? She must know that last year New Holland Agricultural was the Netherland's largest exporter of farm equipment, right? And that the CR Series Tier-4B Twin Rotor Combines were rated as Best in Class in last year's Heavy Equipment Guide? Even Taylor Swift has that song *Buy Your Heavy Tractors, Ploughs and Combines From New Holland Agricultural but Sell Your Heart to Me for A Kiss*. I have to assume she knows as much as me, and I have to plan accordingly. I have to focus.

8

TIME TO CHOOSE an outfit for the 10th Annual Lepidopterology Convention! I am just so excited. If I can anticipate her actions and outfit I could surely make a vivid enough impression on her to erase my past shortcomings. It seems obvious to me that she would be matching heavy artillery with a business casual ensemble. Would it be an M4 Carbine Commando with an Armani Collezioni wool blazer? If so, do I go with twin Colt M1911 9 mm chrome pistols and a Dior herringbone two-piece wool suit? What if she went with an Alexander McQueen tulip sleeve silk mini dress strapped with a classic Heckler and Koch MP5K? It was too ridiculously sexy to think about. Should I then pair a Comme des Garçons slashed two-button sportcoat with a Fabbri hummingbird inlay shotgun? This is too important to fuck up so I go bold. Brioni Men's tonal wool-silk plaid print two-piece suit with a pair of LeBronald Palmer Nikes and a 5.5" barrel MDX 505 PDX with muzzle. I had plucked a couple feathers from the white peacock at St. John the Divine's in the UWS and I place them beneath my white Madewell classic bandana. I look awesome and I'm packing some serious firepower.

The 10th Annual Lepidopterology Convention was originally scheduled to be held at the Jacob Javits Center in midtown, but due to a septic overflow in the effluent sewer system, the event had to be relocated to Rockefeller Center, where there will surely be a VIP event scheduled at Christie's. I feel an enormous sense of pride with a tinge of flattery when I think about the lengths she is willing to go to ensure a successful performance. The reception is set to begin at 7 p.m. with the unveiling of the rare Peacock butterfly at eight.

It's unlikely she will mingle amongst the crowd before the start of her performance. There's too much risk, too much room for error. Could she intelligently discuss the migration patterns of Painted Lady butterflies? Did she know the dormancy period for various pupa stages? I, on the other hand, felt perfectly at ease discussing everything from the extinction of Queen Alexandra's birdwing to caterpillars' cunning mutual association with ants. (By transmitting vibrations through the substrate they are able to lure ants to feed on the honeydew secretions on their back. The sneaky bastard tricks the ant into luring it back to its colony where it feasts on ant larvae.)

I arrive promptly at seven with the intention of lingering around the entrance, in hopes of identifying some of the attendees to the Christie's Auction Week Gala. This is not to be, however, as I am almost instantly greeted by the smiling face of the Resistance artist I have been searching for. She kisses me and hugs me as if we were reunified lovers. She is beaming with joy. She bounces on her heels as if she can barely contain herself. If I wasn't already, I am now completely head over heels for her.

"I'm Ana," she says with an unidentifiable accent.

"I'm Bespoke Downs."

"Is your name really Bespoke? What kind of name is that?"

"A custom one I guess."

I pull the envelope (which had been simply labeled *October 1960*) from the inside breast pocket of my blazer and present it to her. "Aren't you armed? Doesn't seem like there's much room for a rifle in there."

She looks stunning in a formfitting Alexander Wang satin and crepe jumpsuit with a fitted waist and wide legs. She has cut her black hair short and appears younger than I previously believed.

"Oh, I'm so prepared for this, silly."

She takes me by the hand and leads me through the well-dressed crowd. I can smell the very same Carnal Flower perfume that Mr. Koch's dentist's secretary wore floating off of her neck. She no longer reeks of body odor. She is quite obviously more prepared than I gave her credit for, and I am beginning to worry. If she knows about my past clients, what else is she hiding from me? Of course she expected me to recognize the perfume. Maybe she is just being playful? Either way I appreciate the attention to detail.

"Ana," I think to myself. So pretty.

A waiter walks by and she swipes two glasses of champagne from his tray. We toast and she turns deadly serious for a moment. "Once a butterfly emerges from its chrysalis, it has but a short few weeks to live. Do you think that's enough time, Bespoke? Is it enough for the butterfly, I mean? It *is* quite literally, a *lifetime*."

"Yes, I suppose. When you put it that way."

"So you're with me tonight? Do you know the rules of the performance?"

"Of course."

"Are you armed?" she asks. I flash my AR brace pistol. "Good," she says. "It's about to start."

Two men step onto the stage, one of them carrying a domed vitrine with a black shroud draped over it. She turns to me. She places her hands on the small of my back and kisses me warmly. In this extended kiss I feel overcompensation, as if years of love are being forcibly compacted into this very moment. Then I taste remifentanil.

My eyes flash open in complete panic. I clutch at her slender shoulders. My knees go weak and buckle under me. Black spots cloud my vision. She has my gun. A soft caress brushes across my ear as she gently guides me to the floor. Before blacking out, I hear the sounds of her checking the clip in my MDX followed by her shrill but commanding scream.

"On the ground, motherfuckers, before I execute every last one of you!" she screams in a perfect imitation of Amanda Plummer's Honey Bunny.

9

I WAKE UP ON a carpeted stage on the 24th floor of Rockefeller Center, at the Christie's Auction Week Gala. My vision is blurred. Sound is muffled. I can see her snakelike frame moving in front of me, across the stage, weaving her way through easels displaying the merchandise of Orphist masters, commanding the shocked crowd. With one hand, she appears to be dragging something, someone, whose hands are bound behind his back. In her other hand, she holds the shrouded cage. My vision begins to clear and she glances over at me, her smile absolutely radiant. She hurls the terrified man towards me and he smashes face first onto the stage. She lets off a few rounds with my submachine gun, pulls the shroud from the case and holds it high for all to see. The man rolls over and looks me directly in the eyes. "You," he says.

I scuttle back on my ass as I recognize my client, Mr. Wei. His eyes shake with tears and snot runs freely from his nose. I eventually hit the curtain covering the back wall and try to refocus.

Ana releases the rare Peacock butterfly from its cage. Its three-inch wingspan seems eternal as it clumsily pushes its way into the air, gaining five inches, then dropping two, then fluttering its wings to get six more. It is this struggle, beyond the impactful designs and impossible color patterns, that endow these insects with such profound beauty.

Ana starts firing indiscriminately into the crowd. Blossoms

of blood sprout on black tuxedos and evening gowns. The insect flutters around the room. More gunfire. Blood sprays across the artwork as if from a fountain as the would-be bidders scatter for cover. I lie defeated, pressing my cheek on the thin carpet, watching the blood run down the paintings.

I am horrified. She has taken our flirtation way too far. By bringing in Mr. Wei and endangering a potential sale, not to mention throwing out all of the time and effort I'd already invested into the pitch, she's crossed a line. I am heartbroken and infinitely disappointed. My client, his wellbeing and his happiness, is my solemn responsibility. It is a precept of my occupation dating back to Castelli's *9th Street Show* and I'm not about to disappoint my mentors.

Tucked deep inside my silk sock was my beloved suicide gun, my single shot Mauser C77 pistol. One bullet. One purpose. I raise it in the air and take aim at the beautiful rare butterfly. It flaps and rises. It flutters and sinks. I squeeze the trigger.

The butterfly retains its perfect symmetry as its forewings separate from its hindwings. The bullet instantly obliterates the thorax and abdomen but its wings hover in the air, briefly, like shards of stained glass from an exploding church. Then they spin and flutter to the ground and all shooting stops. Ana turns to me.

"What the fuck, B?"

I hear the *pop*, *pop*, *pop* as she severs my spinal column with three 62 x 39 mm slugs. Before mercifully passing out from pain, I see her shake her head and possibly wipe away a tear. I hear the screams filling the room and then the sound of my promising career going to utter waste, before I ever had the chance to offer Mr. Wei Robert Rauschenberg's *Canyon,* 1959. It is painful and loud and it sounds like this. *Pop*.

Chattergun

1

LATE ONE EVENING, a simple and violent man named One Lung Currin was escorting his hideous young wife out of a popular tavern in the neighborhood of Hell's Kitchen. One Lung Currin had chosen as his profession a leadership position in the homicidal street gang known as the Westies, and thus was quite well known to the people out that evening in the chilly November air. He walked with his left arm around his wife, and on his right arm hung her overcoat. When they stepped out into the cool night, the streets still teeming with drunken purpose and corrupt enterprise, he held up the coat and slid it onto his wife's back. She wrapped the lapels tightly around her neck and did a little twirl. The overcoat was an anniversary gift from her maniac husband. He had taken it off the back of a police officer who the Westies had ambushed and brutally assaulted, and had it tailored to fit the feminine fashion of the times, before presenting it to her wrapped in a red bow. The bespoke coat with the violent past was quite the topic of conversation in the Landmark Tavern that night. Mr. Currin was proud and smiled with satisfaction.

"Aye! Dere's dat coont!"

Four police officers, three of them in overcoats, came rushing at One Lung and his wife. One Lung confronted them.

"Ye bek fer mer, eh, cucksuckeh?"

The cops surrounded him. He took a hard blow from a nightstick to the back of his head and was momentarily incapacitated. The coatless officer grabbed Mrs. Currin (number of lungs unknown) and shook her violently until she fell to the sidewalk. She sprung at him like a mountain lion. The officer caught her and slammed her head on the pavement until it cracked. "Coont," he said as he pulled the coat off her. The sound of a dozen revolvers blasted in the air, sending a swarm of bullets into the city sky and people running for cover. The streets were filled with Westies that evening, each one famous for a quick trigger. The gangsters gathered and surrounded the scene. Three of the four cops were executed on the spot. One Lung was helped to his feet by his men. A revolver was put in his hand. The coatless officer was presented to One Lung on his knees. A Westie lieutenant laid the overcoat on top of Mrs. Currin's body as a pool of blood formed a Byzantine halo around her head. One Lung pressed the barrel of the gun to the officer's head.

"Fek yoo."

Boom.

The top of the officer's skull shattered and he fell to the ground with a heavy thud. One Lung stood above his wife's body. People appeared in the doorways of the pubs and tenement buildings, buzzing with curiosity. All, that is, but a woman in a dusty black sarafan with a black felt veil, who seemed to appear on the sidewalk near Currin. In her arms she held the body of a child, its limbs were limp, dangling silhouettes. The men recognized her immediately as the witch Helena Blavatsky. She had a strong reputation for being able to communicate with spirits not of this world. She was the founder of the New York Theosophical Society and many of the Westie's wives sought her counsel. It was said she was able to speak directly to Artio and Epona and travel freely

through the Otherworld. She collapsed to her knees in front
of Currin's dead wife. Madame Blavatsky pulled the tailored
wool coat from the body and wrapped it around the child.
She approached One Lung and, without lifting the veil from
her eyes, raised her arm and pointed behind her, to a third
floor window with a three-inch hole where a stray bullet had
gone through. Not one member of the Westies was versed
on the laws of gravity, and few had more than a modern third
grade education, but that was hardly an excuse for their lack
of foresight when they shot their pistols straight into the air.

"Aye dun wan neh trooba, Misses, just wan me wyfe's
coht," said One Lung Currin.

Madame Blavatsky chanted frantically beneath her veil in
an ancient and foreign tongue. Her grumbling grew louder,
faster and a trail of smoke leaked from her veil like steam
escaping from a boiling kettle. The smoke was an emerald
green and increased in both thickness and intensity as it
flowed from her veil like living hair.

"Yeh wheeytch coont!" One Lung shouted as he ripped
the veil from her face, revealing a pair of furious black eyes.
Her mouth hung open like an exhaust pipe and the mysteri-
ous smoke billowed out. One Lung began choking and fell
to his knees clutching his neck. Madame Blavatsky released
a stream of glowing vomit onto One Lung's head. He sprung
to his feet and stumbled backwards. The green, steam-
ing vomit clung to his face like a parasite as he ran wildly
through the streets. In his mind demons appeared. Animal
spirits howled and roared and hissed so loudly that he lost
all sense and skittered aimlessly to escape their cries. In a
blind sprint he ran over to the piers then turned underneath
the elevated tracks on Eleventh Avenue, clawing at his own
head. People moved out of his way and pointed but dared
not whisper, because ghosts hear whispers.

When he got to the corner of 24th and West Street he
collapsed to the pavement, dead. Kind of.

2

New York City, Present Day

I HAVE SO MUCH FIRE in me and I have so many plans. Born again in fury and ambition. Everything is desperate. Everything is revenge, no matter how petty. Everything hurts, but it's my head that's really fucking killing me. It's like the painful ringing in my ears and the boiling fury in my belly have formed a vise to squeeze my eyeballs out. I'm going to let the anger win. I know anger. I can focus through it. Just. Focus.

Fuck those motherfuckers. I'm going to kill them myself.

The walls in the 10th Precinct interrogation room are made of painted cinder block and rows of large, grey, derelict metal lockers. The floors are linoleum. The ceiling is a typical office-style dropped ceiling with fluorescent fixtures, one in every three actually working. There is a pivoting desk lamp on the table that looks like it was misplaced from its home in a university library. The cuff on my wrist that has me tethered to the table is not very tight. The guard must know that I would have his scalp if it were. My lawyer should be here shortly, but I'm afraid of what I may have already told them. My wife used to say I have a big mouth when angry, and I was fucking furious. When I'm angry, I mean, when the fighting starts, everything sort of changes for me. Everything takes on a saturation of color like it's fake or something. It looks like one of those 3D movies (I just saw my first one. It was four hours long and called *Leap Into The Void* starring Oscar Isaac as Yves Klein).

The police ushered me here under the pretense of taking my statement after they rescued me from the Resistance compound, but this seems wrong. I'm injured, my bottom lip split down the middle, but instead of taking me to Mount Sinai they take me to the Tombs. They found me tied to a chair in a broom closet during the raid on the Resistance compound. Someday I'll kill them all. Those spoiled art school brats staged one of their gestures at the opening reception of my Christian Marclay exhibition. They killed half a dozen of my best clients before I realized their screams weren't just part of a sound collage. It was absolute plunderphonic carnage. I was never particularly unsympathetic to the Resistance, but now they were affecting my bottom line. The conservation charges alone from that massacre will probably set me back this quarter. They ambushed me as I fled the gallery and threw me into a van, right after that fucking weirdo with paint smeared across his nose rolled up to me in his wheelchair and kissed my ring.

That's all I remember of the attack until I woke up at their hideout, duct-taped to a chair, in a room painted entirely with VantaBlack™. The effects of the deep black wall pigment had me momentarily disoriented. I was no longer able to distinguish between the floor and the ceiling. All was lightless and endless around me. I suppose this was intended to be some sort of psychological torment, but I found it quite relaxing. The absence of light combined with the damp stillness in the air gave one the feeling of hovering in a sensory deprivation tank. It reminded me of my time spent dead, and those were peaceful days.

Then the girl came in. I remembered her from the attack on my opening. I was a big score for her. A big fish. I got the impression that she was disobeying orders by speaking to me. They were waiting on the arrival of some equal sized fish, I imagine. But she couldn't help herself and had to sneak a peek. She smelled so offensive that I couldn't have opened my mouth to speak to her if I wanted to.

"James Chattergun," she said, "I can't believe it's you. I've heard so many stories. I mean, the things they say about you..."

The slender girl, possibly Israeli but hard to tell, with cropped hair and a very stylish outfit, shook her head as she pulled up a chair in front of me. Her skin had the hue of day-old newspaper. Her broken English was not high pitched, but annoying nonetheless. It was impossible not to notice the Martin Katz diamond deco bracelet dancing on her wrist, which I had seen before, at the gallery three days prior, on the wrist of Laura Linton. I tried to speak, to tell her the stories she's heard are tame compared to the truth, but a burning spout of stomach acid pushed up my throat when I opened my mouth. I swallowed it and tried to hold my breath.

"Is it true you think you're a time traveler?" she asked.

I started dry heaving, and my neck and shoulders convulsed accordingly. Get angry, I told myself. Focus. My nostrils expanded like gaskets and I drew in the putrid air. I stretched my mouth into a grotesque grimace so that the gash in my lip spread and a tiny balloon of blood sprouted. I exhaled and tiny bubbles of blood escaped through the spaces between my teeth.

"I'm a ghost, sweetheart."

I spat on the table. Her triumphant mannerisms enraged me. I knew I could find a way to kill her despite being tied to a chair in this impossibly black room, but she got up to leave. As she moved backwards towards the door, she appeared to be floating.

"It won't matter if you're a ghost or an alien once David and Gena get their hands on you," she said. "It'll be a spectacle. Society as a hootenanny."

Then came the boom, an explosion in another room,

possibly street level. The girl looked stunned, scared. There were banging sounds, then gunfire. Another explosion knocked her to the floor, which, due to the enigmatic VantaBlack™, I could not distinguish from the ceiling. I rocked back and forth on the chair until I knocked myself on top of her. I clenched my teeth on her cheek and she did the same to mine. She dug her nails into the tendons on the side of my neck. It hurt like a motherfucker. I headbutted her in the jaw. She scrambled to her feet and ran towards the door. She paused for a moment, stabled herself on her high-heeled footwear, pressed her index finger into the center of her forehead and said, "Zen for head, motherfucker."

She slipped out the door, and moments later the room was filled with tear gas and cops. I was rushed into an ambulance, and instead of the hospital I find myself here, in one of the numberless rooms in the lower Manhattan Detention Complex, or simply, the Tombs. This is hardly the first time I've been locked in here. Hell, I was practically raised here. If you could survive here long enough, you were sure to learn many helpful tactics in criminal enterprise. Back in my day, my first life, as me, the Westies always ended up down here. Even though we stayed in Hell's Kitchen most of the time, we'd always jump in for dust-ups against the Nativists. We were tolerated by Tammany because we ran the rackets on the western piers. Things weren't so clear-cut down at Pier 17 near Collect Pond though. Our kinfolk were in a constant state of warfare defending their livelihood and territory. Occasionally we'd head down to crack some Bowery Boy skulls. Whoever survived ended up in the Tombs. It truly was an awful place. Charles Dickens described it in his *Notes on America* as follows: "Ascend the pitch-dark stairs, heedful of a false footing on the trembling boards, and grope your way with me into this wolfish den, where neither ray of light nor breath of air, appears to come." Counterpoint: fuck Charles Dickens.

Anyway, that was a very long time ago, when I was another man. Today it is quite a different story. By some dark sorcery I was born again into the body of New York gallerist James Chattergun, and he feels more like me than I've ever felt. He has the finances I never had, and I have a skill set money can't buy. I've really come to love him, his family, his friends, his money. This love didn't just magically awaken in his body, like I did. It had to be developed, and for that to happen there needed to be some changes. I had to be cruel. Cull the herd. People were resistant, of course, but those who are left are happier now than they ever imagined.

It's been a year to the day since the old James Chattergun, the prominent and respected gallerist, took his own life by swallowing a cyanide capsule on a Chelsea sidewalk. Moments later James Chattergun again opened his eyes, but his mind was mine.

The fact that One Lung Currin reawakened as James Chattergun and no one seemed to notice fills me with a thorough respect for the man. I was quickly the most formidable art dealer in New York City. Hong Kong, Shanghai, Mexico City and Los Angeles soon followed. I owned the largest freeports in Delaware, Ireland, Geneva and the Emirates. I obsessively worked the auction market. I bought and flipped young artists with surgical profitability.

I'd inherited a large roster of established art stars, and I executed half of them shortly after taking over in an attempt to lighten my own workload. I was inspired by an event I barely understood at the time, but it moved me quite profoundly. Three days after my awakening, I was obligated to attend the viewing of John Akomfrah's remake of *Mad Max 3: Beyond Thunderdome*, and it gave me an idea. In his genre bending twist on the 1985 classic, the role of Masterblaster was played by Zendaya sitting on Duane Johnson's shoulders, and their performance was powerful. The duo ran a crude methane refinery in Bartertown, like in the original, but Akomfrah's slow motion camerawork and ultra-high-def image quality combined with the Oscar-worthy performance of Zendaya, made it truly something special when she cried, "Break a deal, face the wheel."

Akomfrah's typically heart wrenching musical score moved like an improvisational gesture, masterfully mixing Ornette Coleman with Bismillah Khan. He had my emotions frantically vibrating like the surface of a tear. It's possible I was still overly emotional from my recent rebirth, but I felt truly inspired when the crowd of onlookers in the makeshift arena known as Thunderdome stomped their feet and shouted, "Two men enter! One man leaves!" I held my kerchief to my nose as Mad Max (this role gave Michael B. Jordan his second "Best Kiss" MTV Movie Award) opened the door of the arena holding Master's pretty severed head.

Put yourself in my shoes. The art world can be very intimidating to newcomers. You tend to speak in a language that is pompous and aristocratic. You say words like *experiential*, *aesthetically*, and *formalism* and it makes me very, very mad. So when I inherited a roster of over forty contemporary artists, I was quickly filled with a specific type of rage that only follows feelings of inadequacy. To me their work looked childish and lazy, at first. I was quick to recognize the precarious nature of my situation and determined to educate myself on fine art aesthetics and the art market. After a brief week as a New York gallerist, I saw my best course of action would be to eliminate a sizable portion of my roster, giving me the dual advantage of limiting the number of egos I had to manage while at the same time upping the existing market value of the artists who unfortunately didn't survive the cutbacks. Ladies and gentlemen, enter the Thunderdome.

I'd placed ads for "Chattergun Fine Arts Presents: *Be! Yonder, Thunderdome!*" in Artnet, Hyperallergic, and ArtNews. I announced that the fighting would end when there were nineteen artists left. To whip up some buzz amongst the blogs I held a lottery to invite two young artists to join Thunderdome. Congratulations Chase Hall and Kye Christensen-Knowles. Aesthetically, it was a bloodbath. The gallery was packed beyond capacity the night of the performance. Even the Resistance were there, strictly as onlookers, admirers I used to think. The arena consisted of a repurposed version of Richard Serra's *TTI London*, 2007. The Baer Faxt reported the performance as follows: Rachel Whiteread disembowelled David Altmejd with a three-foot shard of quartz crystal. Sean Landers managed to kill Gilbert before being strangled by George. Nick Cave showed up in a soundsuit with a chainsaw. George Condo achieved the highest body count with four. Tied in second place were Rita Ackermann and Roxy Paine with three kills each. Raymond Pettibon's death, while technically in the arena, was of unrelated causes.

The next morning everything was the same, but simpler, more streamlined. Over the course of the next few weeks I scheduled one-on-one meetings with the surviving artists at my favorite restaurants. We discussed their work in depth and made aggressive exhibition plans. There was much confusion as to why I felt the need to reintroduce myself, and why I spoke with such a vulgar Irish accent (which I've since learned to suppress, for business reasons). I made it a point to exercise an act of extreme cruelty right before the close of each meeting, so that my dedication to my artists was clear, and every one of them wholeheartedly bought into my agenda. For instance, I commonly brought in a member of the waiter or waitress' family and executed them on the spot as they brought out our dessert. The tiramisu at Café Boulud is divine.

3

THE DOOR TO THE NYPD interrogation room creaks open and in walks Seymour Solomon, my lawyer, followed by two plainclothes police officers. I immediately realize that the role of bad cop would be played by the hefty female detective, a dead-eyed grandma with two katana swords strapped to her back. The tall bald gentleman with insightful eyes in the two-button suit must be the good cop. They pull up seats across from me. My lawyer wastes no time expressing his concern and indignation.

"My god James, are you alright?" Seymour moans, then turns his attention to the detectives. "Why is he being detained? You have him chained like a goddamn criminal!"

"We are following up on credible intel," says Detective Fowler, good cop, as he leans forward on his elbows. "We're going to need Mr. Chattergun here to fill in some blanks."

"I don't gotta tell you anything, pig."

"It's ok, James. Please, trust me. You can tell them the truth, everything," my lawyer assures me.

"Fuck these pigs, Seymour. Since when do we cooperate?"

"It's part of the immunity deal. Total transparency."

"You've changed, Seymour. I hardly recognize you."

I'm suspicious, and suspicion makes me mad. "Since when do you advo-fucking-cate for co-opo-fuck-a-rating?" I get eloquent when angry. I begin banging my chained right hand up and down on the table. It shakes with every hit. I let out a scream and hold it until my lungs are empty. The officers are speechless and I hear Mr. Solomon sniffle.

I breathe in deeply through my nose and ask, "What would you like to know?"

"Tell us about the attack at the Christian Marclay opening, Jim. You masterminded the whole thing, right? Tell us how you coordinated with the fucking Resistance. Or was it a false flag event? You think we're fucking stupid, don't you, pencil dick? How many of the victims did you owe money to? We're subpoenaing your financials as we speak, bitch. Within a week a grand jury will be examining the inventory in your freeports, so time is not on your side. But if you spill it all now, you may just be able to save yourself," says Detective Warner, bad cop, as she taps her nails on the table. "But let me be clear, shitbird," she continues, "you leave out any detail and the immunity deal disappears."

"First off, if you ever use my familiar name again I'll rip out your tongue. Secondly, it began like any other opening day. It was hectic right from the start. Security woke up my wife and I at 5:00 a.m., normal time. She watched me work out, like every morning, squirming on the bed with lust and anticipation as my deltoids grew and my pectorals flexed with every sweaty rep, until I finished my routine and made passionate love to her. We had breakfast in the sunroom at 5:15 and my attention was immediately focused on the Eastern markets, which would be closing shortly. I checked on the status of payments, because lateness is not tolerated. Then my morning touch base with Semion Mogilevich, Director of MMOMA and every gallery in Winzavod, Moscow. Like I said, it was like every other day. Jerome and Landry, my guards, were waiting outside with the car, as always, when I kissed Lewanne goodbye and headed into work."

"Was there anything out of the ordinary on your way in? Anything at all?"

"Not really. Well, Landry was driving, and Jerome was in the back with me. It was only strange because it seemed to me as if they thought I wouldn't notice. They're twins, you see? Strange ones, with their braids and bracelets. But they are stone cold killers when you need them to be. They told me why they dress that way, but I can't remember. Something about some singer, Milli Bonilli? Anyway, Jerome always drives, it was a little strange he didn't. But it was even stranger that neither of them mentioned it until I brought it up."

"Hold up," says Warner. "They dress like 80s pop stars and it didn't ring any alarms for you?"

"What the fuck are you on about?" I grunt. "I don't waste my time following the trends of fucking kids. I call them, and they drive me. Or, I call them, and they kill. End of story."

"How long have they been your security?"

"About six months. My security personnel don't live very long. But they're paid well. The fella before them lasted two weeks before he was beheaded in a Michael Asher performance. So six months is good for me, and they are good kids. There was traffic on Fifth Ave, but the NYPD escort flanking my car pushed us right through, so it wasn't a bother. Midtown was messy due to the riots at the Folk Art Museum, but once we got to the West Side Highway it was fine.

"I made phone calls and Jerome took notes. I spoke with Becky Mercer, Warren Kanders, Alice Walton and Fritz Dietl. Oh, and MBS and Kush WhatsApped in. Usually I'm at the gallery at 10 a.m. sharp but that day we were a bit early. I remember because my best salesperson, Nigel Bridge, was sprawled backwards on the reception desk, eating out the cleaning lady, who was straddling his face, while also fucking a sales associate, who fumbled to unlock the door amidst the rear pounding. I patted his belly as I strolled through the cacophonous Marclay installation and readied myself for my morning viewing of Anslem Keiffer's *Maria durch den Dornwald ging*, 1992.

"I was not looking forward to this viewing because I had a deep connection with this work and was reluctant to part with it. The clients, Mr. and Mrs. Gruen, would have to work extra hard to get me to agree to sell this masterpiece. They owned half a dozen Keifers already, and their reticence to make an offer on this one was beginning to irk me.

"My assistant was waiting for me outside my office. Security unlocked the door and scanned for bugs or other listening devices. I sat at my desk and she ran through the itinerary, but I was distracted by the lighting on a large Francis Bacon diptych, which needed adjusting. I don't really know my assistant, but she seems competent. She never forgets to crush a Dexedrine in my coffee, and sometimes slips me two."

"Cute story. Let's walk through that itinerary, eh?"

"What? Watch your tone, asshole. Where was I? Oh yeah, the fucking Keifer viewing with the Gruens. It went good. I didn't sell it though. But, and I truly hope this is the case, I believe I've managed to expose Mr. Gruen as the senseless twaddle that he truly is, and I hope that the lovely Mrs. Gruen will find a more worthy man for a husband. It would fill me with joy to see that whip-smart octogenarian reinvent herself in a more refined marital state. I was *this* close to selling it to him, to breaking my own heart, but when he let it slip that he intended to install it on a wall adjacent to an Ian Davenport, I immediately flipped the razor blade I had stowed in my gums outward between my teeth and rushed at him. In a flash I was up on his lapels, pressing the blade against his neck, on the verge of drawing blood. My face burrowed in his neck, with the blade deathly still between my teeth, I grunted, 'I believe in the empty spaces. They're the most wonderful thing.'

"When he began sobbing, the blade started breaking through his saggy, thin skin. I inhaled deeply through my nose, saliva and a little blood streaming from the corners of my mouth, and got ready to slice his neck wide open, but I was snapped to attention when I heard the cries of the worldly Mrs. Gruen.

"'You're a fucking pussy, Harold! Come on you little bitch, fight back!' She was furious. I relaxed my jaw, and the blade plunked to the ground. She continued, 'You ain't gonna do shit because you ain't shit. I fucked Benny, Harold. Oh yes, that part of him still works. Works great. Now either fight like an actual *art collector* or just slink away like the limp dick bitch you are.'

"After the viewing, I was hungry so I had a chicken breast. I had a conference call with Roman from the Garage in Moscow followed by a Zoom chat with Stefan Simchowitz. Afterwards, I went to meet Christian Marclay for lunch, to talk about our strategy for the evening. He was keen to push through a museum acquisition, but I had bigger plans. You see, POTUS was a big admirer, of mine, not Marclays, and I knew his art advisor would be coming to the opening. I wanted to place Christian's installation in the bedroom at Camp David. I was planning on convincing him at our lunch meeting, but Christian never showed. Goddamn artists. I figured since I had a table at Del Posto I might as well eat. I went prix fixe. I asked my driver to go outside to find someone on their lunch break to eat with me. He came back with a young man from Woodside, Queens. Two kids. Works construction. 'Eat up,' I said. 'Enjoy.' He devoured the spicy lamb and chestnut ravioli. Two glasses of Barbaresco and tartufi al mascarpone. He was glowing. 'Close your eyes,' I said, then left. I was already in my Beemer when the check arrived."

"Did you ever find out why Mr. Marclay didn't show?" Detective Warner asked.

"No, never did. He better not have been at lunch with Larry. I got back to the gallery and had a few glasses of John Powers during a sales meeting. Some of the sales staff stayed around after to fuck, then I went to change clothes for the evening. I keep a penthouse apartment in the old Anglican Seminary on 20th Street."

"Quit fucking stalling, Chattergun," Fowler scowled before

Warner interjected.

"I'd like to hear more about the seminary, if you don't mind."

"Nah, the Seminary's got nothing to do with this. Next question," I say.

"It's ok, James. Tell them what they want to know," my lawyer assures me. I don't like it, but Seymour has been my counsel since shortly after my *awakening* and I trust him as much as anybody.

"I don't live in the Seminary, for security reasons, but it is the only place in this city that still feels like home. After an unfortunate series of accidents removed the previous tenants, I took it over with Larry, DZ, Arnie, Marc and a couple of the other gallery boys. We lease the old converted condo area to the Vincenzo Peruggia School to use as dormitories for one of their campuses. They're a wild bunch. The rest of it was divided up into viewing rooms with adjoining Emergency Rooms on the first floor and penthouse apartments for all of New York's top gallerists on the upper floors. The ERs are fully equipped with a trauma center, a drug counseling center and a psychological recuperation wing. Their immediate proximity to the viewing rooms allows our salespeople the ability to use more aggressive sales techniques without fear of losing a client to injuries or madness. The viewing rooms themselves are gorgeous: 25 foot high ceilings with arching skylights, a one inch reveal above the four inch polished walnut floor planks, adjustable LED track lighting and so much more. The Episcopalian cathedral has been transformed into virtual reality viewing ambulatories and chapels. All of the pews are equipped with Titan 11K Cinematic 360 VR allowing clients to visit distant exhibitions and art fairs. Contrary to common expectations, a crowd of well-dressed art lovers deeply engaged in an isolated and solitary aesthetic experience has a distinct holiness of its own. There is a deep solemnity when they slide onto their knees and light the votive candle in front of their viewing pew, our notice that an offer has been made. That was David's idea. The ventilation system pumps in a heavy stream of oxygenated air, but most of our clients are already loaded from whatever narcotic they purchased from the dense crowd of drug dealers packing the sidewalk on 20th Street. That was my idea.

"The Seminary is now the center of New York's fine art trade. It is constantly buzzing with activity. I based the idea off of the Old Brewery on the Bowery back in my day. Back then all illicit business went through the Brewery. The Five Points boys were ruthless and nothing got done without them getting a taste. The Seminary now functions in much the same way. There are secret entrances and exits located all over the complex so VIP clients come and go unnoticed. There are both crypto and traditional currency exchange stations throughout. The existing red brick structure is now just a façade covering twelve-inch steel walls. The 19th century mosaic window depicting the risen Christ has been remade from ballistic stained glass. GagWater runs security of course, but I keep my own gang of killers and sales professionals. Are you getting all this?"

"Quit jerking us around, old man," says Detective Fowler. "Everybody knows that shit. Come on, tell us something we don't know. Where'd you go from the Seminary?"

"Nowhere."

"James, the truth. You went to dinner, right?"

"Jesus fuck, Seymour. So what? It was just dinner. People gotta eat. It was perfectly normal. We had to discuss sales strategy for Christian's show. Quite boring, really."

"Cut the shit, Chattergun. We got tapes. And so far, you haven't told us anything that would stop us from putting your ass on ice," says the increasingly infuriated Detective Fowler.

"Who's the fucking rat?" I yell and slam my palm on the table. "It's gotta be Gavin, right? I shoulda buried his ass under his stupid glowing dance floor years ago."

"Jesus, James," Seymour says. "The restaurant was bugged. Mr. Chow's has been under surveillance for years. Ever since Mayor Nixon had the rest of the *Sex and the City* cast poisoned there. You should know that."

Detective Warner stands up and takes a deep pull from his vape pen. He lets out a very large cloud of thick, strawberry scented smoke and says, "We just need you to identify some voices for us. Just need confirmation. Remember, if you fucking lie to us we'll know, and you'll regret it." He pulls a recorder from his pocket and presses play.

Once the last of the Rohingya are resettled, we will begin breaking ground for DIA Myanmar.

"Fuck you!" I say. I think back to that dinner and how excited my good friend Leonard Riggio looked when he told us that news. I, like everyone else, was quite terrified of the man and would be loath to cross him. The detective presses play again.

The success of the coup has sent El Anatsui's market sky high. Cough. Cough. And the Administration has been receptive to the idea of a long-term installation along the US/Mexico southern border wall. Who wants to hit this?

"Fuck you," I say again and smile to myself. Jack Shainman surely has enough dirt on me to have me extradited to Ghana to stand trial for crimes against humanity, so I was not about to rat him out. The detective presses play one more time.

If you make something good and interesting and not ridiculing someone or being offensive, the creators of the original material will like it.

"Oh, that was Christian Marclay. He was joking, obviously," I say.

4

THE DOOR TO THE interrogation room creaks open again. An elderly Japanese woman leans her head in but does not enter. "Five minutes," she says. "They just arrived."

Seymour drops his head into his hands. The two officers stand up. Something's wrong. I don't know who they are expecting but it's got to be someone important. Maybe someone from the State Department or Secretary Deripaska himself? My lawyer reaches into his pocket and drags out his phone. He is trembling. He holds up the screen so that I can see it and plays a video. I see his wife and two cats duct-taped to a wicker chair. The wife whimpers and the cats make their horrible sounds. The fetid young girl who tried to interrogate me earlier at the Resistance compound leans into frame. In her hands is a cordless DeWalt reciprocating saw. She squeezes the trigger and the 5-inch blade shakes violently. The video ends in a blurry still frame of his wife's neck, her pearl necklace tangled in the tightly wound duct tape.

"My god, Seymour," I said, "What the fuck have you done?"

Seymour sobs openly. He is a pitiful man. My family is safe because I am feared. He puts his own family in danger through cowardice. Now he has me imperiled by it as well. *Cowardice is the worst of all vices*, the devil once told me.

"I had no choice," he whimpers.

The door swings open but no one enters. The two detectives straighten their clothes in anticipation. The threshold dims. In walks a tall, handsome man in his seventies. I recognize him immediately as one of the most wanted men in America, one of the two Resistance bosses. He is wearing a form fitting dashiki with an exotic bird print and has two belts of ammunition crossed beneath a Ketepa corded necklace.

"David motherfucking Hammons. I've been looking for you, sir."

"Well, how you like me now, bitch?" David Hammons proclaims. My lawyer and the detectives can't help but applaud at these lines, which have become a very famous catchphrase for Mr. Hammons. David Hammons had become quite the gadfly of the Resistance, but he was a dangerous man. I knew that if he was here, Gena couldn't be far behind. She wasn't nearly as reasonable as Hammons, or so legend has it. Very few survive an introduction to Gena Rowlands.

"Well, I'm here. So say what you gotta say, old man," I scowl defiantly.

"A couple of years ago, James, if that's what I should call you, you bid up my *African American Flag*, 1990, to a ridiculous twelve million dollars above reserve. That was a bitch move, James. Should I call you James, James? What if I called you One Lung? Would you respond to One Lung?"

"Aye. Wuld answer t'dat es will. But if'n ya wanna tek ta Wan Loong, yer gunna hevta dell wit im ta da ind."

A guard wraps his forearm around my throat and squeezes. David raises his hand, and the guard releases his grip. I choke and cough and desperately gasp for air.

"I don't give a shit who you think you are, Mr. Chattergun, but I do want information. We want access to your Delaware freeport storage. I'm willing to work with you, but Gena has other plans. She imagines staging a grand tableau on Tenth Avenue. I don't know the details, but she did mention Chris Burden's birthday the other day so I don't imagine it'll be any fun for you. If, however, you can make yourself valuable, it may just save your life."

"Gu feck yerrself, coont. Shuyt meh en de arym err ney-hl meh ta a Vuuhlweegen boog, aye dunt cayrr," I say. The guards shuffle restlessly around me. The door bursts open and in walks Gena Rowlands, actress turned Resistance performer, reluctant leader turned willing enforcer. In defiance of her years, she moves with the sleek determination of a mountain lion. Everybody in the room snaps to attention, save for myself and David, who turns away as if an opportunity was lost. "Hello Gena," he says.

"Hi David. I see you and Mr. Chattergun here have begun getting acquainted. No? Not James Chattergun? Could it be Mr. One Lung Currin?" She is toying with me right off the bat. "I need James Chattergun. So please, Mr. Lung, fuck off."

"Hey baby," I smile.

"Cut the shit, James. This is it, dude. I'm the motherfucking closer in your grand denouement," Gena Rowlands smiles back. She continues, "Looking at your exhibition history, the last three years alone should be enough to put you in The Hague. Check out these numbers coming straight from the Admin itself." She hands me a sheet of paper that reads:

Exhibition	Promotion Casualties	Installation/ Shipping Casualties	Opening Reception Casualties	Exhibition Duration Casualties	Total Lives Lost
Franz West "WarHeads/ LemurHeads"	4	11	9	19	43
Richard Serra "Cor-ten Steel Against Humanity"	12	49	19	27	107
Roman Signer "Arbeiten mit blud vor dem Met Museum"	3	7	12	38	60
Louise Bourgeois "Passage dangereux"	40	23	19	80	162

"Well, you can't make an omelet, sweetheart," I say. I raise my jaw proudly in anticipation of a punch as she clenches her fist and hurls it at me, complete with a four-hole knuckleduster. It rips my cheek and cracks two molars but does not break my jaw. I spit blood onto the table, raise my eyes and say, "My people, they may not know how to read, but they sure like those pretty pictures." This time it is David Hammons who strikes, slicing my brow line with a Turkana finger hook. It takes me a bit longer to recover but when I do, I look him directly in the eyes.

"Why, Dave?" I say. "It's over. It's been over since the Third Administration. You think you're going to change things with your art? You think you're going to bring elections back? Or do you still think the bubble is going to burst?" I can't contain myself. I laugh until I cough.

"Everybody out," Gena says. My lawyer, the guards, and the two detectives leave the room. Gena walks over to the lockers along the wall. She runs her long, finely polished fingernails along the faded metal doors as she slowly paces the room. She pauses and turns to me. She raises her right fist and slams it against the locker.

"Do you think we're playing, James?" She raises her fist and pounds the locker again, this time in three decisive thuds. Another banging follows, frantic and panicked, coming now from inside the locker. I can hear muffled screaming. Gena turns the dial on the combination lock and releases the mechanism. The dented metal door swings open, and the exhausted body of theosophist Helena Blavatsky flops out. Gena Rowlands swiftly kicks her in the ribs, two of which are already broken. The witch Blavatsky is bloody and disheveled, but doesn't look a day older than the night she encountered me and my gang many years ago. She is wearing the same torn black sarafan she wore when we first met, but the thick felt veil is gone.

"Jesus Christ, Gena," David Hammons moans. "Chris

Burden? Really?"

"*Five Days in a Locker Piece*, 1971," she says. "I'd like to do more than five days, but that's the performance."

I shouldn't be, but I am quite surprised. She must be over 140 years old and she hasn't aged a day. In fact, she is younger looking than I remember. For the first time in half a century, I'm afraid. The Resistance must know more about me than I previously thought. My fatal flaw is underestimation. I don't dare let my concern show.

"I'd like some chow mein," I say.

"Eto vi," Blavatsky growls.

The witch gathers herself slowly, but does not get off her knees. I truly applaud her stubbornness, despite my mocking laughter. Drops of blood and sweat fall from her brow to the floor. I stop laughing. "Coont" I say. "Shuyda kilt ye."

"Come back, James," demands David.

"I'm here, bitch."

David raises his right hand, fingers straight but together, and holds it high in the air with a slight cup to the palm. His arm comes down on me hard. "How." Smack. "Do." Smack. "You." Smack. "Like." Smack. "Me." Pause. "Mother-fuck-ing now." Smack. Everything goes black. I regain consciousness with my cheek pressed against the linoleum floor.

"Goddamnit, DH!" Gena is annoyed. "I was going to tell him my plan."

"Tell him your plan? What are you, a fucking super villain?"

"You know," Gena says, "my husband John and I were originally set to direct and star in *Octopussy*, respectively, back when Peter Falk was slated to play 007, but we backed out when Falk was dropped for refusing corrective eye surgery. True story."

"Well, what do we do with them now?"

Gena lifts her leg up and holds her right knee high in the air. The tread on her jungle boot is thick and deep. It lands cruelly on the forehead of Helena Blavatsky, knocking her unconscious. She takes a moment to compose herself and adjusts the collar of her blouse. Ever so beautiful, she says, "On with the plan, Stan."

5

A SLENDER WOMAN rhythmically strides down a sidewalk on a brisk autumn day. She is confident in her heeled leather pumps and high-waisted jeans. She wears her cashmere sweater as a second skin, equally comfortable and sexy. The orange-tinged September sun worships her swollen lips. People passing by all take a moment to appreciate her focus and gait.

She does a cute little bounce-step as a long black snake slithers by her designer footwear. She smiles and flips her hair. Another black snake slithers by. She does a little hopscotch dance. The way she confidently glides through life's hassles with poise and decorum is impressive. Black snakes start slithering by in multitudes. They are up to her ankles. Soon it is a stream of slick, black snakes. She is successful and strong. They are up to her knees. She is fearless and exceptional. It is a tidal bore of slimy black snakes up to her waist. She works hard, and plays harder. A wave of snakes slither around her elbows. She is sophisticated and chic. The snakes are up to her neck. She turns to the camera. She gives a knowing smirk.

"When, exactly, did you forget what makes you special? Fifteen minutes can save you fifteen percent. Geico."

6

I WAKE UP IN A COLD, converted warehouse, on some shitty couch, energized but seriously disoriented. My vision is blurry. The TV is on, and there's a stinging sensation in my right elbow. I'm slightly horny from the last commercial. I grind my dick into the cushions for a moment and think to myself, *James Chattercunt, you're so much stronger than these pussies will ever know*. I'm not tired. I never am.

My suit is missing, but I've still got on my briefs and socks and undershirt. I'd be a little self-conscious, but it is a modest enough ensemble in which to kill some people, which is exactly what I plan to do. I'm ready to go. *Fuck*. My legs don't move. My arms don't either. I lift my head but I don't. *Fuck*. I can see, but in double, triple, blurry. I see the light of a door opening at the end of the large room. Around me I hear voices, talking, laughing, mocking.

Two men pick me up by my arms and drag my limp legs through a gauntlet of cheering Resistance members. It is a veritable who's who of famous artists, anarchists and rogues mixed among scores of fashionable, young Resisters. I see John Lurie toasting with Ta-Nehisi Coates and Gerard Malanga. Jenny Holzer has Jello Biafra playfully in a headlock. Nari Ward, Colin Kaepernick and Black Thought are laughing about something. Richard Tuttle and Glenn O'Brien are waiting for Brian Eno to pop open a champagne bottle. I see Christian Marclay arm in arm with Rachel Maddow, laughing and pointing at me. I am surely high on some psychotropic substance and things are getting weird. Spirits of the dead seem to be walking among the living. James Baldwin chats with Jim Carroll and Mike Kelley. Andrea Rosen laughs hysterically as Felix Gonzales-Torres does his famous Carlton from *Fresh Prince* impression. Malick Sidibe teaches Sergei Polunin a two-step. Anthony Bourdain is hitting on Nadya Tolokonnikova as Kurt Vonnegut shows a secret handshake to Claude Simaurd. Kara Walker, Kerry James Marshall and Barkley Hendrix attempt to start a wave. Louise Bourgeois and Claus Oldenberg are trying to get a game of spin the bottle going but Fran Lebowitz is not amused. Lawrence Weiner is scribbling something on the wall with René Ricard and Mikhail Bulgakov. The narcotics overcome me and the rest is a blur until I pass out again.

When I wake, I feel the refreshing cold touch of finely polished stone on my ear and cheek. I've felt this impossibly smooth chill many times, but usually after an orgy with the staff. I'm definitely in an art gallery, which could be a good or bad thing, but it is preferable to a parking garage or the base of a bridge. A hazy figure pulls a needle out of my arm, which is now covered in track marks. I feel woozy. I tell myself, *I'm not tired; I nev—* My forehead hits the concrete and my vision goes out.

7

FOR THE FIRST TIME in my life, I wake up on my feet, in a full tuxedo, with a cocktail in hand, in mid-conversation with Iwan Wirth. I'm at an opening reception and he is trying to explain something to me about a collector named Thanos and an artist named Tony Stark, I think, but I'm finding it hard to follow. I scan the room. Nothing seems to be out of the ordinary. Finely dressed clients with heavily armed security forces are milling about. Sales people rush to and fro, attending to clients as they wave their heavy, black credit cards. Influencers pose for selfies too close to the artworks.

I see large Hellenistic statues, in perfect snowfall white, holding blue glass orbs. Shit, it appears to be a Jeff Koons show. I see large marble effigies of Demeter, the Centaur, Diana and Apollo looming among the finely dressed crowd, cradling the reflective glass balls as if they contained humanity's most fragile desires. The Resistance loathes Koons and accuses him of profiteering. I loathe him as well but accuse him only of simple-mindedness. Whatever the Resistance has planned, I am sure to play a central role.

"Mr. Chattergun, Sir. May I have a word with you? Apologies, Mr. Wirth."

It's my salesperson, Nigel Bridge. I'm thrilled to see him.

"Nigel," I say. "What the fuck is going on here, lad?"

"Was gonna ask you the same, Sir. Where the fuck you been, Sir?"

"The cunts had me. The Resistance bastards. Until the cops

stormed the place. But they weren't really cops I suppose…"

"Yes. The cops raided the Resistance compound, they rescued many dealers and collectors, but you weren't one of them."

"Hmm," I say. "How's your family, Nige? Got any recent photos?"

"This one's from today," he says as he pulls out his phone and scrolls through his photo roll. "This is Meegan eating cheesy mac."

"That's fucking disgusting," I say.

Good, I think to myself, Nigel is a strong man. His family is safe because he is feared. I can count on Ni…

"You ok, Nigel?"

He clenches his eyes shut seemingly in pain. "Nige," I say. "It was just a joke, man." He opens his eyes and they are solid black orbs, endless and terrifying, similar to the effect of the VantaBlack™, or like the blank eyes on a Modigliani nude. He grabs me by the shoulders with an unnatural strength and spins me around, so that I'm facing the cavernous exhibition space. All fall silent. I am confronted with a sea of those endless, black, terrifying eyes lodged inside the faces of the art-loving crowd. Their heads are turned to me, but it's impossible to say where they are looking. Every expression is blank and lifeless.

As if guided by remote control, they move as one, zombielike and slow, the crowd separating to create a pathway in front of me. At the end of the pathway stands Helena Blavatsky, flanked by David Hammons and Gena Rowlands. Hammons is dressed, for some reason, like Fidel Castro, head to toe in olive green, with an eleven-pound Cuban gold chain around his neck. Gena is in a classic wrap dress. But, perhaps most shocking of all, the witch Blavatsky looks young, radiant and royal. Behind them, a crowd of Resistance performers gather.

A zombie collector absentmindedly walks up to a statue

of *Crouching Venus*, 2013, and picks up the large blue orb. He turns and carries it through the crowd and into the path cleared between myself and Blavatsky. He raises it high above his head and smashes it onto the cold, polished stone floor before slowly rejoining the idiot crowd. Another zombie collector does the same. One by one, an orb is removed from the lap/hand/head of a statue, carried solemnly to the path, and smashed on the floor. In a matter of minutes, every orb has been demolished and a path of jagged, cruel shards of glass lay before me.

I am exhausted, but it is clear to me what must be done. I loosen my bowtie and unbutton my starched white shirt. I slip my jacket off, followed by my shirt. I unbuckle my belt and kick off my shoes. *Thank you, Gena*, I think to myself. I need this. I need pain. I need this performative rebirth. And she is giving me the chance. I stand in front of the shattered glass in nothing but my silk boxers. I clasp my arms behind my back and fall to my knees.

Chris Burden, *Through The Night Softly,* 1973.

I fall forward onto my chest and the jagged glass pierces my skin. Pain like I've never felt before. I shift my body weight onto my left shoulder, then heave myself forward onto my right. Lightning shoots through my body. *The price of Conceptual art's entry into polite society is surrender of its abrasiveness and anomalousness.* I shift my weight again, and flop forward another few inches. Blood is starting to spread across the floor from my shoulders, chest, and knees. I am crying, grunting, screaming and lunging forward with every ounce of strength I can muster. *The world is full of objects, more or less interesting. I do not wish to add more.* I squirm, pitifully but pridefully across the gallery floor. After a while, it no longer hurts. My chest and stomach are completely shredded but I am a king. I look down at my torn flesh and I'm reminded of the Soutine painting that my wife Lewanne bought me for our anniversary. I smile and crawl even faster. *I do not mind objects, but I do not care to make them.* I reach the end of the painful glass pathway and weep openly at the feet of my enemies.

I feel a pair of strong hands pull me up from my armpits. I am weeping on my knees. I am not tired. I never am. I close my eyes and whisper.

"I don't know if I'm making myself clear, but if I were to accept this business of Conceptual art, I would have no reason to exist."

The invisible hands pull me to my feet.

Madame Blavatsky is glowing. For real, she's glowing. She looks as glamorous, if not more so, than any woman here. I am drawn to her. Once again, like steam escaping from a kettle, a torrent of green smoke begins to leak from her mouth. I feel blissful and boundless, above death but under heaven. The smoke from her mouth is now thick and flowing. She raises her jaw and stretches her arms. She releases a stream of fluorescent vomit on me, like she did on that night all those years ago. I am again on my knees. All around me is still... soundless... fading. As the world shrinks and then disappears, I hear the witch say, "Nu vse, tebe pizda, One Lung Currin, poshyel k chyertu."

8

WHEN I WAKE IN the hospital my loyal wife Lewanne is asleep on the chair beside me. I feel like I've slept for an eternity. There is a breathing tube in my throat and my body is completely wrapped in bandages. I don't feel any pain but my thoughts are foggy. I remember I was under investigation by the SEC and wanted by Interpol. The last thing I remember clearly is taking a cyanide capsule that Nigel gave me but after that my memory is blank. Sort of. I feel traumatized, but I'm not sure why. I can't speak. I'm scared. The curtain to my room is pulled back and in walk an elderly couple. For a moment they stand silhouetted at the threshold, then they enter my room. The man is tall and the woman elegant.

"It's him, David. It's the real James Chattergun. He's back," the woman says. "We've got him."

Diviner

1

MY STORY COMES WITH many caveats, so let's just dive right in. This is an earnest attempt to bring some context to any forthcoming allegations. Believe me, this is as earnest as I know how. *Earnest Goes to Camp. Earnest Saves Christmas. Earnest Scared Stupid* and, of course, *Earnest Goes to Jail.* This is my truth and it is only slightly more valid than others simply due to my recognition of the cautions below. It is as much about art as art is about anything. It is as much about love as love is about paint, stone, bronze, steel, plastic, canvas, blood and words. Above all, believe me, it is as much about love as love is primarily about performance. Worth less than worthless, but still my most valuable possession, my story cannot begin until we have made some things clear.

Caveat 1. The following is only as reliable as my memory permits. Not in some Proustian, "Rachel when from the Lord" way, but more in a *Mulholland Drive*, post-traumatic mosaic of freak-fest actors and plotlines way. It is the memory of a man who is not the same man who made the memory in the first place. My memories live in the mind of a man who is, first and foremost, motivated by feelings of shame and self-loathing that pin me to the bed in the morning and sit on my shoulders through the day. The man who made these memories, however, was a man of action, every morning propelled through the day with a sense of destiny and edification. That man is no longer with us. RIP. VIP. RSVP.

Caveat 2. Culture, in its wide and variable forms that have

furloughed the arrangements of the past, has an accelerated responsibility to commercialism, and as such, the artists and authorities need to accelerate both their production and their consumption. The increased debasement of civilizing tenets has enabled a perennial disaster in intellectual and artistic practices. We all are, to a great extent, accomplices to the dominant order, because we cannot reject it without rejecting the concept of *culture* as a whole.

Caveat 3. Although I recognize the fact that my decision to show exclusively through Chattergun Fine Arts was motivated by a desire for fame and fortune, there were other forces at work. An unseen hand was arranging the scene, setting the stage. Through press reports, public trials and depositions, I've since learned my decision was of great interest to multinational corporate interests. You could imagine my surprise. I was ten years removed from my MFA show and, erringly yet *earnestly*, I believed my success to be well earned.

Caveat 4. There will always be an avenue of artistic exploration that exists solely to explore the context of its own right to exist. Any attempt to invalidate the analysis of artists whose singular pursuit is to illustrate their own actuality should be looked at as counterrevolutionary recontextualization and will be added to any forthcoming list of charges.

Caveat 5. When I told her I wanted to take a break I was just bluffing. Much like Ross and Rachel in Season 3 Episode 15, I've since come to regret it. But baby, you really should have known.

Tomorrow I open a major painting show at one of New York's premier galleries, and I need to get my story straight. So, here it is, my tale, as the actress said to the bishop.

2

TRUE LOVE IS BEST viewed in hard shafts of warm, raking light, and the best light is, of course, Caravaggio's. I met Ana at the Gallerie d'Italia—Palazzo Zevallos Stigliano in Naples. I was standing in a crowd of tourists gazing at the 17th century masterpiece *Martirio di Sant'Orsola,* 1610. Suddenly the camera-clad sightseers in comfortable shoes dispersed and I was alone for a moment, until she appeared, wobbling like a baby horse on sleek, leather heels. She was gorgeous and she chewed her gum loudly and was exactly what I was trying to get away from.

"Looks like shit," she said. "Fucking shame."

"Ok," I said.

"Marcantonio Doria. Spoiled dago rich kid who just couldn't wait for the paint to dry." She laid her fingers across my arm. "It was damaged in transit from Caravaggio's studio to his goddamn Villa. Probably so he could get his holy dick wet while hosting some pervy masquerade ball." She grabbed my arm as I turned to flee. "Some things shouldn't be rushed."

"I'm sorry. I don't speak English."

"Come on, man." She pulled me closer and gestured to the painting, which floated on the wall like a late summer sun. "Check out how uneven the varnish is. Look at the pale color pallet. It's super fucked."

"It's one of maybe forty Caravaggios in the world, but still, totally cool to bitch about it to a complete stranger, I guess." I couldn't let her challenge go unanswered. She smiled.

"It is a tribute to a bad bitch."

"Who? Saint Ursula?"

"Yeah, a total babe too. Refused to marry the King of the Huns and took an arrow in the chest for it. I'm Ana. Ana the Hun."

Ana had a dour way about her. Very bleak. Like Diana Davila's character in Woody Allen's *Play It Again, Sam*, from the art gallery scene, but fancier, kind of. She wore a sequin evening dress with a wrinkled Army jacket and a trucker hat that read "Ballroom Marfa." She had a backpack slung over one shoulder.

"This was it, you know, his last painting before he died of lead poisoning. Or murder. I'm Ray," I said, "Ray Diviner."

"What do you say, Ray Diviner? Wanna go see *The Seven Works of Mercy*? With me? It's just a few blocks away."

"I probably don't think that's a great idea."

"For you or me? For all I know you could be some *Talented Mr. Ripley* type psychopath hiding out on the coast."

I was a big fan of the writer Patricia Highsmith and considered for a minute telling an anecdote I had heard about her bringing a handbag containing a head of lettuce and a hundred snails to a house party but then I thought Ana was probably just referring to the shitty 1999 film that inexplicably earned Jude Law an Oscar nod.

"Yes," I said to Ana, "Let's go."

We spent the rest of the day together but in the evening she disappeared. That was fine by me, really. Gold TV Italia was playing a marathon of the first ten *Simpsons* seasons, back when Gaia Bolognesi was still doing Bart's Italian voice-over. She will always be the true voice of Italian Bartman to me and I was eager to soak it in. When I ran into Ana the next morning, she was in quite a state.

We met for coffee at a café in Santa Lucia. She spent five minutes arguing with the baristas about giving us two Americanos "to go." I was a bit surprised by the scene she was making and that she seemed unconcerned about looking like a tourist but honestly, she was absolutely right. Arguing with Italians about taking your coffee to go gets old after the second day. And who wants to linger around a coffee bar with strangers anyway? I was struck, however, by the fact that she argued in English. I had assumed her to be Italian.

"You don't speak Italian?" I asked as she tottered towards me with two espressos in hand. She was dressed exactly like Ana Karina from *Bande à part*, although I didn't realize it at the time.

"No, silly. Why would you think I speak Italian? Here, smell this Caffè Americano."

"Oh, I can't smell. I mean, I don't have a sense of smell. Where is your accent from?"

"Huh, that makes sense. What accent?"

We both adored the city of Naples and its crooked charm. It brought out a certain wild side to our burgeoning love. The winding alleys forced long, deep shadows across the cracked concrete in defiance of the daily splash of orange sunlight, and it made us feel alive. Ghosts of pirates, sailors, scoundrels, artists and whores cluttered the southern ports and fueled our adventures. She stayed in my room at the Eurostar Excelsior on the waterfront for the rest of my trip. When we weren't out visiting museums, or drinking and eating and drinking some more, we were in my room, enjoying that uniquely unbridled type of sex inspired by fancy hotels. I made it a point to only turn on the TV when she fell asleep, which was often, so I knew my feelings for this girl must be true and strong. I flew home before her, but we eagerly made plans to continue our relationship one week later in New York.

3

THE WEEK I SPENT in the city before she returned was heart-wrenching and endless. We hadn't exchanged any information at all, no phone numbers, Facebook or Insta. Instead, we had made plans to meet on the park-side entrance to The Frick on October 10. I don't think we were trying to add intrigue to our romance, but I do think we were searching for a way to make it uncommon, to rip it from all the undistinguished origin stories in the quilt of modern love. Of course, it wasn't the most original idea, and the whole thing had *Before Sunrise* vibes to it, but I'm quick to forgive my own corniness.

My trip to Italy was designed to help me find some clarity. I had recently agreed to an exclusive sales deal with Chattergun FA, and I had some reservations. I had been happy at CANADA gallery, but after Phil Grauer was exposed as Q, the shadowy leader of the right wing conspiracy group, I lost my passion for showing there. Although I hadn't met James Chattergun himself, I'd been hounded by his team of sexy artist liaisons since my Harvard MFA show. The truth is I wanted to be famous and I wanted to be rich. Two weeks ago, I had met with Chattergun's top salesman, Nigel Bridge, at his office in CFA's 24th Street space. Immediately following the meeting I took an Uber up to JFK and was on the next plane to Naples. The conversation with Mr. Bridge can be found below.

"Listen, boy, right now you got money. You got enough

independence to pick and choose representation, where and when to show your work even, but you don't have *Fuck You* money, and that's what you're here for, no?"

"What?"

"*Fuck You* money, boy. Choose your collectors. Choose your institutions. Get out of art blogs and into the pages of a high-gloss Phaidon edition. Influence world leaders through prime placement. Tickle the brains of children on their class trips to museums. Real power, Ray. Real power."

"Yeah, ok. Is that like a Burt Reynolds thing? I don't really think much about power. I mean, it's cool if that's your thing, Mr. Bridge..."

"Please. Nigel."

"It's cool if that's your thing, Nigel, but really I just want the money. Did you see my auction sales? I just want in on the big dollars, Nigel."

"Sure. You want to use the secondary market to lift your primary market. Absolutely fair. We'd like to move forward, Ray. Our winter programming has cleared up significantly and we'd like to move forward with a solo show in the New Year. *Chattergun Fine Arts Presents: Ray Miller Diviner.*"

"Fuck. What? As in January? Like...soon?"

"Is that a problem?"

At this point, Nigel Bridge snapped his fingers and four artist liaisons entered the room, instantly filling it with an overpowering cornucopia of scents from the Barney's fragrance counter, which was of no consequence to me, of course, except for the fact that strong perfume makes my eyes water. It is typical for galleries to hire seductive liaisons to keep their artists happy, but the liaisons at Chattergun were known to be extraordinary. Young men and woman in sexy, couture outfits modeled after Victorian prostitutes make up the bulk of their liaison staff. They also have specialists employed for artists with specific sexual requirements. This is information I am privy to but will keep confidential, out of respect. Girls in short bustle skirts, corsets and wigs huddled around me in fawning admiration.

"You see, Ray, we've already set you up at a studio in Gowanus. There's a car out front waiting to take you there now, in fact. You have an assistant waiting for you as well, stretching and priming canvases as we speak. What do you say, Ray Diviner?"

I said yes. Nigel walked me out of his office, through the Sam Gilliam exhibition in the gallery, and to the black Escalade waiting in the light rain outside. The driver opened the door, and Nigel grabbed my arm as I was about to get in.

"Listen to me. Money, fame, popularity, all serve to establish cultural authenticity. People don't have an appetite for complexity. What they crave is bold, basic, visceral intensity. Ok, now be a good lad and get some painting done, eh?"

He directed the driver to take me to my new studio, with its freshly primed canvases lying in wait. I directed the driver to take me to JFK airport where I hopped on Alitalia Flight 182 to Naples.

On the flight back to New York, I didn't feel like I had any fresh perspective, but I was eager to get to work. Truthfully, I wasn't really going through some existential crisis making this decision. I'd always assumed I'd be represented by one of the major galleries. It was clearly on my trajectory and fell perfectly within my timeline. I am barely a decade removed from getting my MFA. I've had successful group and solo shows, a solo pavilion at Frieze, attended Skowhegan, Chinati, La Napoule, and I won the goddamn Roma Prize. No, I wasn't going through any existential crisis at all. That doesn't mean there weren't a myriad of other psychological monsters waiting to sabotage my life.

I had a general idea of the type of paintings I was going to make for the show. Yes, they were going to be large. Very large. No, I was not going to change my style. I was going to keep making the same paintings I've always made. My entire career has consisted of these "Fly-Eyes"—two ovoid canvases with hundreds of hexagonal shapes emanating from their centers in a rough approximation of flies' eyes. Hard, black lines define the internal angles of the polygons, which lie upon areas of gestural abstraction, thick impasto or distressed canvas, where the reflection in the eye is inferred. When I began creating these works, I did not refer to them in this way. I was clumsily exploring a Western reinterpretation of Islamic sacred geometry, multiplying shapes by divine proportion as described by Carl Friedrich Gauss and Johannes Kepler. It was only in Roberta Smith's review of my first major solo show that the term "Fly-Eyes" became the go-to nomenclature, which I quickly embraced for its absurdity. Of course, I tweak my themes and arrangements for every installation, often employing motifs for certain bodies of work, but I had no intention of straying from what had brought me this far.

From the airport, I went directly to the studio where I found my new assistant asleep on the couch surrounded by dozens of stretched and primed canvases. It was 5 a.m. and I startled the hell out of both of us. His name, I learned, is Sosa Mendez, and he was a 19-year old recent dropout from Cooper Union. Sosa rubbed the sleep from his eyes and ran his hands through his shaggy, curly black hair. He shook my hand and told me he is deaf in his left ear. "It's ok," I said, "I can't smell."

Sosa flicked the light switch on the wall, and a dozen industrial pendant lamps cast a cool glow in the spacious warehouse studio. Large windows covered the south wall and provided a view of the Carroll Street Bridge in front of monstrous shipping hoists. Sosa flicked another switch and rows of LED track lighting cast an even spray of white light across large, plaster walls. It was absolutely amazing. Sosa gathered his things into a backpack.

"Bathroom's over there. Couch, obviously. Record player. Books. Records. Bluetooth system. Kitchen over there."

"Where's the…"

"TV? Check this out."

Sosa picked up the remote control from the coffee table and pressed a large button. Two large panels on the wall, disguised as a Richard Serra diptych, separated slowly, noiselessly, and revealed a 64" high-definition smart TV. Full streaming, live TV and old-school Cable. He handed me a set of keys. "Big one opens the outside doors. Little one is for the freight elevator, and the futuristic looking one is for the studio. I'll be back at noon tomorrow to get started. Cool?"

"I might take the day off tomorrow. Watch some TV," I said.

"All good by me, but I gotta be here to get paid. The gallery pays me to be here from noon to midnight whether you're working or not. "

"Really?"

"Come on, boy!" He shouted and patted his palm on his thigh. A fat, short bulldog came loping out from behind the couch. "Hope you don't mind dogs," Sosa said and left the door open as he walked out of the room.

I slept on the couch and dreamt that I had one large breast in the center of my chest. When I awoke, the TV was playing MSNBC. I watched the first hour of Morning Willie, but Mika Brzezinski-Geist just spent that time fawning over her co-host and new husband. I smoked a joint and watched the BBC for a bit before putting on the battle scene from *Battlestar Galactica* Season 2 Episode 11. I fell asleep and woke up to the rumbling sound of the freight elevator, opening directly into my studio. The heavy steel elevator door was painted grey, with considerable rust spots on the edges, and made a loud, clacking sound as Sosa heaved it open. He looked awesome as he stood silhouetted in front of a bare light bulb, towing behind him a cart of supplies. Sosa is like a teenage Mexican male version of Mathilde from *The Professional*. He's pretty unique. Dresses like a Lost Boy, and you always feel like he is studying you. Not necessarily looking for a weakness. Not necessarily *not* looking for a weakness.

The fat little bulldog was already asleep in the elevator car.

"What's his name?"

"Behemoth."

"You just gonna leave him in the elevator like that?"

"I stopped by the store and picked up some shit. Got an assortment of Old Holland Classic oil paints, baby! Love their uncompromising adherence to traditional fucking techniques and standards. Gimme that deep 17th century shit, man. Grinding the pigment with stone, by hand. Not some metal roller bullshit. Binding made of cold-pressed linseed oil. That's what I'm talking about."

"What?"

"You see the stretchers? Simon Lui, motherfucker!"

"That's impossible," I said and pulled myself off the couch. I leaned one of the oval shaped canvases forward. "No shit," I said as I ran my forefinger against the distinctive Simon Lui brand, "Where the fuck'd you get this? They've been underground for years now. Are these black market?"

"I know people at the L'exchange markets. Let me know if you need anything. For real, anything."

I hadn't been down in L'exchange for quite a few years. I was way too high profile to be seen at the black markets. The abandoned L train lines were abandoned in name only. Inside they were teeming with criminal enterprise. The city was supposed to reopen them after they quelled the "Culture Tax Riots" but never got around to it. All sorts of contraband moves through the tunnels. Drug dealers and whores, of course, but more interesting are the dealers of black market electronics, weaponry, antiquities and art. The Gallery Boys only do deals here through intermediaries, or sometimes art advisers. The Resistance are allowed to operate here but the relationship is tenuous. The true order in L'exchange is anarchy, pure and simple. There is a madness that swims through the tunnels like a giant, invisible electric eel. Sometimes it brushes by the wrong person's leg and the laws of the tunnel will change. The eel of madness may curl around the toe of a Somali heavy artillery dealer and the laws of the tunnel will change again. Sometimes it discharges its maniacal electro-plaques at a level of 800 volts of psycho-current and the whole tunnel erupts in madness. I'd feel bad asking Sosa to get me weed in such a dangerous place, but if he was going there anyway…

Sosa emptied his shopping cart. Beneath the expensive paint were an assortment of contraband items including but not limited to: a video box set of Derek Jarman films, a VCR player, a DVD box set of Cassavettes films and an external disk player. None of these movies are streaming these days, obviously. He had a milk crate full of records, fucking good ones. Some NY punk like Johnny Thunders and Television, some Factory Records vinyl, an Aphex Twin double set, some Eno and Fripp, Roxy Music, Fela and some Afrobeat compilations, all around a pretty good selection for working in the studio. He had a copy of Harold Rosenberg's recently discovered and instantly banned diaries. He had a stack of very old Russian auction catalogs with lots for Adolf Milman, El Lissitzky, Mikhail Matyushin and Naum Gabo, along with two books on Wasily Kandinsky. I didn't do any work that day but Sosa still got paid.

4

MY HESITATION ABOUT dealing with Chattergun was due to reasons completely unrelated to feelings of self-worth. The moral compasses of the other big galleries were hardly true north, but Chattergun was off the map entirely. GagWater is probably the most globally impactful of the galleries, Boeing Art-Supermarket NYC is the most heavily involved in money laundering, but James Chattergun is known for two things, and they both involve taking people's money. Since it was money that I was after most, at the time, it was an obvious choice. Also, they were quite desperate for living artists, as they had lost two thirds of their roster at a *Mad Max 3: Beyond Thunderdome* inspired performance event a few months ago.

I wasn't very concerned about legacy. I was all for prestige in the *here and now*. It doesn't matter to me how future generations will view my work because honestly, I'm not convinced there will be a future generation. This studio will be part of the East River in a decade. Who the fuck knows if the NYC water is really safe to drink? There are countless nuclear weapons with varying degrees of stability being stored around the world. Just here in the States, moving east to west, we are getting increasingly stronger and more frequent hurricanes, tornadoes, earthquakes, and wildfires. The major religions of the world take turns through the centuries leading the charge for murder and martyrdom. Over twenty years ago, I watched the towers fall from the corner of Broadway and Canal with a cluster of hickies on my neck so believe me, I am not concerned about legacy at all.

I've read enough biographies of men and women smarter and more talented than me, whose names were lost to the broad strokes of posterity, to hold onto any hope of being revered through time. I've probably never even heard of the best of them. You neither. The annals of history are mostly random, and randomness is mostly cruel. There will never be a righteous attribution of worth and truth in history no matter how deeply you Google. The truth is the pretender king was not pretending. The truth is the con. The truth is a master fraud and the truth is rarely necessary. Tomorrow is Tuesday, I think, but who fucking cares?

Sosa said it was Wednesday when he woke me on the couch. I could feel a heavy depression looming over me even after he poured two cups of coffee and put on McCartney's underrated *Red Rose Speedway*. I turned on CNN but quickly muted the TV. I tried to pretend I was going to do some work today.

"Feeling great," I said.

"No doubt. Big day today."

"What?"

"The sales staff from the gallery are coming by to see your progress. Probably talk price points. At 2:00. So...two hours. I think they're gonna be really impressed," he said sarcastically.

"Fuck you," I said. "I'm gonna get some air. I'll be back in a bit."

I quickly fell into my jeans and slipped on a hoodie before my overcoat. I stood by the large metal elevator doors and patted myself down to be sure I had phone, keys, wallet. When I heard the unmistakable thud of the arriving freight car, I unlatched the doors and heaved them open. Inside the elevator was Behemoth, sleeping soundly on a brand new plush doggie bed. Impressive. I reached street level and stumbled quickly down the avenue, as if I had somewhere to go.

I turned onto 10th Street and into a coffee house.

"Cortado, please," I said without looking up. "To go."

"Oh my god. You're Ray Miller Diviner, right?" The barista was so small I almost didn't see her. "I saw your show at the New Museum before it burned. It was ok. I feel like you depend too heavily on anthropomorphology. Almost like you handicap yourself."

"Actually, I'd like a large iced Americano. Biggest you got. Cuarenta."

I left as quickly as I could. I sat on a bench, rolled a ciggie and tried to figure out what the fuck I was going to do. I was reminded of what Omar said on Season 1 Episode 8 of *The Wire*. "The game is out there. It's either play or get played." He was absolutely right. Put me in, coach, or some shit like that. It was late autumn and getting cold, and I had no idea, really, what the theme of my show would be, or exactly how I would tweak my recipe for maximum effectiveness. In all of my daydreams, I could vividly picture every detail of the opening reception. I knew who would be there. What they'd be wearing. I could imagine which collectors would cluster with which dealers and which journalists would be huddling with which museum directors. It was beautiful. I could even envision myself sitting cross-legged, with a blazer over my Dead Kennedys t-shirt, responding to questions from an eager Jerry Saltz across a greasy linoleum table top in my favorite Mexican diner. The only things I could not picture in my mind, unfortunately, were the actual paintings. Nothing to freak out about though. I know what I'm doing.

I've given up on the idea of fame as currency. I've moved on to the gold standard. Some nights I dream that Lucy Lippard appears in my bedroom doorway. She's wearing a bed sheet over her head like a ghost, but my erection tells me it's her. She moves slowly and climbs into bed with me. I am extremely turned on by the sheet, but I dare not move as she holds her head to my ear. I can feel her breath, so hot that I imagine it reeks, and she whispers, "Looking at and appreciating art in this century has been understood as an instrument of upward social mobility, in which owning art is the ultimate step. Making art is the bottom of the scale." I awake agglutinative and fatigued, but wholly indoctrinated in the veracity of her pillow talk. I am working my way up the hierarchy. By aligning myself to an ideologically hip intellectual piety steeped in Foucault, Derrida and Adorno, I am by implication a vehicle for the more vacuous privileged classes to exhibit their pet aptitudes. My product is recognizable and my myth is familiar. I am lifting my metaphorical sneaker to a higher rung on the social ladder, which ends in wealth. Wealth and an impressive art collection.

Sufficiently angered by my ruminations I rushed back to my studio. "Sosa!" I yelled as I stormed into the room. "How'd you paint these walls? I mean, did you roll them or spray them?"

"Boss, they gonna be here in a minute. You should probably get your shit together."

"You sprayed them right? How much we got left over? For real. Don't fuck with me right now."

"We got plenty. I planned on putting on a fresh coat once a week until Showtime."

"Get the sprayer. Load it up."

I quickly stowed my overcoat, hoodie and sneakers in the bathroom. Sosa returned with the sprayer, complete with a five-gallon tub of Ben Moore Decorator's White. He passed me the wand and stepped back. "You don't have to stay, Sosa. I'll wait for them," I said.

"Oh man," he said. The buzzer rang.

"Wait," I said and took a deep breath. It rang again. "OK, buzz them in."

I raised the nose of the long, thin wand high into the air. I squeezed the trigger and a cloud of vaporized acrylic paint streamed into the air. I waved the rod side to side as if I was John Rambo blasting rounds at commies. The room was quickly filled with dense, acrylic fog. When everything was swallowed by the thick opaque white, I swung open the studio door and appeared covered in the white paint, taking the gallery entourage by surprise. The entourage consisted of that bastard Nigel Bridge, Natalie his assistant, and three gallery liaisons dressed in tight pink corsets, fur coats and stockings with their hair dyed various primary colors. They all took a step back from the doorway as I emerged from the paint cloud. I was dripping in the flat Decorator's White.

"Nigel! What's up, brother? Please, come on in. You're gonna be psyched."

Nigel Bridge looked down at his finely pressed Dior suit. He looked back at me.

"Fancy a pint instead?"

We went to the Tavern and I was immediately embarrassed by these assholes, but I was sly enough to play my part. I was still completely covered in the white paint, everywhere except my hoodie, overcoat and trainers. Two of the artist liaisons went right ahead and started making out in a booth. The other one fetched some drinks as I sat with Nigel and Natalie. I was unnecessarily cold to Natalie, the eager and capable assistant, but only because I wanted her to feel it more deeply when I was kind. Nigel I treated like an idiot, and it would take an oral treatise on international tax law from him to convince me to treat him otherwise.

Nigel cut out a few lines of coke on the table and passed me a two-inch straw. I held it between my thumb and forefinger and asked him, "Can you reduce your beliefs and presuppositions, and everything about your character that you hold dear down to their most elementary particles? A conceptual thinker believes in nothing other than their own existence, and nothing except their relation to space, and the objects that disorder it. A conceptual thinker is smothered under an avalanche of redundancies. Do you think you author your own experience, Nigel?"

"What are you on about, chap?"

"All I'm saying is, you want it to be one way, but it's the other way."

"I'm sorry, what?" Natalie chimed in.

"Boy, you got me confused with a man who repeats himself," I said to her, triumphantly.

I put the little straw into my pint glass and sucked down the cold pilsner in one go, straining and twisting my neck to get the final drops. I returned the straw to him and asked for another pint.

"We're starting you off at 500k per tondo'" Nigel said. "We'd like eight paintings, minimum."

"They're diptychs, Mr. Bridge. Gotta get 800k, minimum."

"Would you be willing to allow studio visits from some of our most important collectors?" Natalie asked confidently. "And...we could easily get a million for commissioned portraits."

"Of whom?" I asked.

"I'll get you a list of potential interests."

Natalie was impressing me, and I was beginning to fear she had uncovered my hidden money lust. I knew the offer would still be on the table, even as I said, "Some fat, rich, fuck gonna pay a mil for a Fly Eye portrait like some renaissance benefactor? You think I'm ready to whore myself out? Should I go stand on the fucking corner? Make an online profile?" I was laying it on a bit thick but fuck it. I finished the second pint and excused myself to the restroom.

I didn't realize until after I had flopped my cock from my jeans that Nigel had followed me into the restroom. I didn't notice at all, in fact, until he thrust my forehead into the hard tile wall by punching me squarely in the back of my head. Pain shot through my skull, my nose. Tears filled my eyes. He pressed my face against the tiled wall with a force that I didn't think he was capable of. My neck began to stiffen and the pain increased. Worst of all, my naked penis rubbed against the urinal wall, the back one.

"You think you can fuck with James Chattergun, boy? We are the worst motherfuckers you will ever meet. When we go to hell it'll be through the front door, understand? You're going to do what you're told. Now wash the fuck up."

I heard the door close behind me. I got myself together as best as I could, but couldn't stop a few hacking sobs out of faint-hearted self-pity and cowardice. I looked in the graffiti covered mirror and saw my reflection between stickers and scribbled tags. I was pitiful. I looked ridiculous. My face and hair were still coated in thick white paint, and a stream of red blood ran down my forehead and wove across my nose. There were two flesh colored streaks beneath my eyes, where the tears had wiped away the paint like dried river beds.

I joined the group at the booth and there was a fresh pint waiting for me.

"Pass me that straw, eh, Nige?"

I devoured three lines of blow from the barroom table. When I lifted my eyes and snorted loudly, the blood began to flow again from my forehead. Two drops landed in the ghostly cocaine residue.

"Natalie, I'd love to hear more about your ideas for portrait commissions," I said.

5

IT WAS A HAZY 58 degrees when I waited on Fifth Avenue for Ana. The only people who stared at the streak of dried white paint dripped over my head were the tourists. It had been three days since that bastard Bridge threatened me, and I had been shaken more than I cared to admit. I had started a daily ritual of pouring a spoonful of white paint over my forehead, letting it run between my eyes and into my mouth, mimicking the splatter of blood that sprouted from my forehead that day in the restroom with Nige. It was my version of the tribal war paint of Roman Gaul, but it didn't make me feel any stronger. Maybe there were other psychological forces at work. Maybe I was trying to scare Ana away. Maybe it was closer in meaning, subconsciously, to the Hare Krishna Tilaka. Or maybe it most accurately resembled the smiley face with a bullet hole, which dripped red blood across a cartoon yellow smile on the cover of the *Watchmen* graphic novel. Regardless, I hated this weather and was anxious to see Ana again.

I had to be careful not to reveal too much of my true nature. I was hiding a man with deep insecurities behind a projected image of an inspired artist. I'd only recently met Ana, but I was instantly vigilant of my thoughts and feelings. It is common to project traits onto people when one is desperately in need of those particular attributes. I was in need of strength and Ana became strong. I was in need of genius and Ana became a singular type of brilliance. But the truth of the matter was that I knew very little about her at all. I knew that she was aggressive, clever, and beautiful. Uncommonly beautiful. I knew she was manipulative, but I was easily manipulated anyway, so most of the women in my life tended to be that way. I had a sense that I could repurpose her, harness some of her energy to get me over the finish line. I always romanticized the idea of an inspired, lunatic passion and believed it could conjure greatness, like fire, through friction. I envisioned us like Lee Krasner and Jackson Pollack, or something.

I saw her flopping up Fifth Ave in an oversized parka and Wallabees, with the slouching posture of an al dente noodle. She looked like she was leaving a Madchester rave-up in 1986. She didn't hug me when she said hello, nor did she look in my eyes. She made no mention of the stream of dried paint on my nose and forehead. I was flooded with self-doubt. I was expecting much more affection, possibly joy, maybe lust. She looked bored and stared at her phone. I panicked.

"How was your flight?"

Before she could answer I came to my senses. I could feel something special about Ana and I wasn't going to fuck up my chances with lazy, prosaic conversation.

"Fuck this," I said.

Ana looked up from her phone. I had her attention but I was struggling for a clever follow-up. I hesitated, then said, "I guess I could be pretty pissed off about what happened to me but it's hard to stay mad when there's so much beauty in the world. Sometimes I feel like I'm seeing it all at once, and it's too much; my heart fills up like a balloon about to burst. And then I remember to relax, and stop trying to hold onto it. And then it flows through me like rain, and I can't feel anything but gratitude—for every single moment of my stupid, little life. You have no idea what I'm talking about, I'm sure. But don't worry, you will someday."

"Wait. What do you mean? What happened to you?"

I was relieved at her reply because it seemed she didn't realize that I was quoting Alan Ball's script for Sam Mendes' multiple Academy Award winning film *American Beauty*. But I needed to give her an answer.

"So much has happened to me, baby." I called her baby for the first time. It was a bold move on my part. "Let me explain everything to you in front of Turner's *Fishing Boats Entering Calais Harbor*, 1805." I took her hand and turned us past the wrought iron gates and through the finely manicured courtyard of the Frick Museum.

Ana hesitated when we approached the metal detectors, specially designed by a descendent of Thomas Hastings, but she passed through after only a couple of tries. When we got to the facial recognition software, however, her face went white with fear. I stepped up to the scanner first, a modified Tony Oursler installation, and looked directly into its cold, metallic gaze. "Hello, Mr....Ray...Miller...Diviner. Welcome to the Frick Collection," the AI security officer announced through a speaker in its aluminum face. I stepped past the scanners and turned to Ana. She shook her head. The look in her eyes was dead serious. Two hulking security guards turned their attention to us. One of them approached.

"It's ok, baby. I'm sure you're not contagious anymore," I said. The security guard stopped in his tracks. Ana sneezed into her hands and wiped them on her jacket. "No, I'm fine," she said. "I really want to see Goya's... cough... *The Forge*... eighteen... cough... cough... twenty-five."

I glanced at the security guard and gave an expression that implied exasperation and annoyance. "Let's get you home," I said and walked her back through the gilded-age courtyard and onto Fifth Ave. When we got to the sidewalk, Ana beamed with joy. "That was good thinking. You're fun, Ray. Ever been to Rief's? Up on 92nd?" I hadn't and I told her so. We both lit cigarettes and walked north on Fifth Ave, on the park side. She didn't answer any questions on our walk up to the bar, not about the rest of her trip to Italy, not about her past, her family, but she was very curious about my past, and she did talk quite a bit about art. I told her of my childhood in Teaneck, NJ. How my adoptive father was a firefighter who was not interested in art at all. We were not wealthy, but my father always found a way to pay for the finest art education, well above his means. It was almost as if an invisible hand had been guiding me towards a career in art. She also showed a strong interest in my studio practice and was incessant with her questions about my exhibition plans and my relationship with my new mega-gallery. We got to the dimly lit dive bar and pulled up chairs to a high-top table in the corner. I looked around the grimy, one room bar, with pale yellow panel walls and a tobacco stained drop ceiling, and it reminded me of New York in the early '00s. The room was full of midday drinkers. A few lonely men, hovered over their neat cocktails, were interspersed with college types and groups of wealthy, young professionals. Ana took a swig from a bottle of Heineken, and the questions continued.

"Are you gonna be rich, Ray?"

"We'll see."

"Have you actually met James Chattergun?"

"He's been in the hospital since I've been taken on. I've had a phone conversation but it was very brief. He's been pretty low-key since that meltdown at that Jeff Koons opening. I was there, you know?"

"Oh my god, me too!"

"Really? I don't remember seeing you. I feel like you are someone I would've noticed."

"Aw that's sweet. I looked kinda different that night. I was going through a thing. Tell me about the Fly Eye paintings."

"I've been doing Fly-Eyes for as long as I can remember. For real. Even in grade school I drew twin, pixelated ovals in the margins of my textbooks. In college at NYU, I settled on using six-hundred-sixty-six cells in each eye, because I thought it was funny, but I've also done series of seven-hundred-seventy-seven cells per eye, four-hundred-twenty, and one-hundred-thirty-eight in my Glen Danzig inspired works. People have always seemed to respond to them. Something about repetition appeals to the human mind."

"Yes, but the fact that they are 'eyes' staring at you gives them a confrontational quality that most Op-art lacks."

"Op-art? I don't know about that, sweetheart, but yeah, otherwise that's very cool. I like that a lot."

"I like you, Ray."

"You too, Ana the Hun."

"How's it going in the studio? You gonna be ready?"

"Honestly, not great. I mean, once I really get going, they'll practically paint themselves. But Nigel has other ideas. He wants me to take commissions, portraits."

"Nigel? Nigel Bridge? You know that motherfucker? He's like, the worst dude, right? Who does he want you to paint portraits of?"

"Yeah he's my sales lead at the gallery. But I'm not really sure who would sit for the portraits. High dollar clients, I'm sure."

"That sounds like a wonderful idea. Really. You should definitely take those commissions."

I was surprised at her reaction, and in retrospect it should have sounded an alarm bell, but I was desperate for a solution, and Ana's support gave me cover to take the easiest and most profitable path to completing my exhibition. That was it. On Monday I would call Nigel, or maybe Natalie, and tell them yes, I'll accept commissions.

"You'll keep me posted, right? About who you'll paint? I just think it's fascinating," Ana said.

Just then, we were interrupted by a group of very drunk young men. One of the boys, a tall, thin, stylish dude in a designer bomber jacket slammed both of his hands on the table and exclaimed, "Ana! What are you doing here? Where the fuck have you been?"

Ana placed her face in her hands and shook her head. "Go away, Darren. I'm not really in the mood for any of your shit." Darren and another man pulled up chairs to the table. "And what's your name, sir?" He asked me.

"I'm Ray." I nodded but did not shake hands.

"Of course you are," Darren said, "Ana's a fan, no? Are you signing autographs?"

"Cut the shit," Ana growled.

"Tell me, Ray, has Ana mentioned anything about the Gleaners?"

The man who had joined us repeated the word "Gleaners" after Darren. It was odd and cultish.

"*The Gleaners?*" I asked, "as in Van Gogh?"

"*The Gleaners,*" said Darren, "as in Jean-Francois Millet."

"It is…was…what we called our performance art group. We recreated famous Fluxus performances in contemporary settings, with contemporary interpretations. But I'm done. Absolutely done with these fools," Ana said.

"Let me buy you a drink, Ray. But first, tell me, when weighing technological determinism, do you feel like cultural globalism is still a useful notion today, considering it's not manifested completely or evenly in cultures around the world?"

"Not when you have societies dedicated to an ideology that is fundamentally universalist. I'd say technological determinism is best used as a marker, eventually but inevitably spawning drastic similarities in seemingly different cultures, globally. At least, that's what I think."

"I think you may be right, Ray," Darren conceded, artificially. He continued, "Why don't we leave these two love birds alone? Don't be a stranger now, Miss Ana." The two men made a show of their departure. I found it quite irritating.

"Damn, they suck," I said, "Who the fuck were those dudes?"

Ana was quiet and still. She looked shook, but only momentarily. Like an actress at an audition, her face changed dramatically when she said, "It's ok, I'm used to guys drooling over me. It started when I was about twelve. I'd go out to dinner with my parents. Every Thursday night. Red Lobster. And every guy there would stare at me when I walked in. And I knew what they were thinking. And I liked it. If people I don't even know look at me and want to fuck me, it means I really have a shot at being a model. Which is great, because there's nothing worse in life than being ordinary."

She was quoting Mena Suvari's character from *American Beauty* back at me. It was a perfect move to end my questions and put me in my place. I texted Sosa that I was bringing someone back to the studio and that he should go run some errands or something, which he did. We didn't have sex even though I tried. We fell asleep together on the large, sectional couch watching HBO's 2003 Mike Nichols directed mini-series, *Angels In America*, which I had a bootleg torrent of (I watch it every December 1, on Roy Cohen Day). We were still asleep on the couch when Sosa came back.

6

THE FREIGHT ELEVATOR doors opened with their usual clank and thud and in walked Sosa with his shopping cart, this time loaded with groceries and toiletries. I heard him whisper, "Goodbye, Behemoth. Be a good boy, ok?" The dog, now wearing a puffy down vest on his new big bed, nestled his nose into his elbows in response. Sosa headed directly for the cabinets and began unloading the cart. Ana pulled the blanket over her head and I threw a t-shirt on top of her. Sosa was not making any effort at being quiet.

"Figured I might as well stock up on some food considering you're practically living here. And some bathroom stuff. Honestly, I don't see how you've been brushing your teeth. Got PB&J, wheat bread, tortillas, a couple bags of shredded cheese, black beans, pintos. I got some frozen dinners and pizzas that'll probably be ok in the toaster oven...Jesus fucking Christ what the fuck is *she* doing here?"

Sosa turned around right as Ana stood and slipped a white V-neck over her head. She was equally indignant.

"Oh no, you motherfucker. You're a fucking dead man."

Ana swiftly flung a ceramic ashtray (that had been gifted to me years ago by Arlene Schechet) clear across the room and into Sosa's forehead. It was quite the feat of marksmanship. Sosa clutched at his head and crouched over. A trickle of blood leaked from between his fingers. Ana dove into her purse and pulled out a small revolver. She cocked the trigger and took two steps towards the boy. Sosa composed himself, puffed out his chest and raised his jaw defiantly. I stepped between them and held my arms straight out to the side, separating them. My head jolted back and forth. "What the fuck?!" I yelled repeatedly.

"He's a GagWater hack, Ray. A fucking freelancer. You can't trust him," Ana shouted and took another step forward.

"Ray, Jesus. How well do you know this girl? Do you know she's Resistance? A fucking psycho too."

"Aw, you know my work," Ana said mockingly.

"Ana," I implored, "put the gun down. Whatever the fuck is going on, we can figure it out."

"Ask her about her *performances*, man. They're massacres. Her re-enactment of *I Like America, America Likes Me* was absolutely chilling. Ask her about the *Fluxkits*, addressed from Jorge McCunias to the United Nations that contained vials of ebola spores. She's wanted by Interpol, dude."

"Says the mercenary scab, shill for *the man*. You got blood on your hands too, kid." Ana turned her attention to me, "Ray, my love, we are better off without him," Ana said, then pulled the trigger. The hammer snapped down but no bullet fired, so she squeezed the trigger again. Then again. "Hey," I said, shamefully quoting James Dean from *Rebel Without a Cause*, "I've got the bullets."

"Ok," Ana said, "We can probably talk this out."

One of my most troubling character flaws has always been an abundance of empathy. I have a hard time getting truly angry with someone. Of course I've been mad before, most often when I've felt damage to my pride, but generally, I relate so easily to my adversaries that I almost instantly forgive them. I think it is telling in regards to my own personal moral codes. As in, I have no problem picturing myself doing the most awful things, were I confronted with certain situations, so I hardly feel qualified to pass any verdicts. It is mostly luck, I feel, which draws the final judgment on our convictions. My luck may change one day. It probably will. Until then, however, my life will be one of near Augustinian virtue. I looked at Ana and Sosa and felt myself a worthy mediator.

The three of us sat down on the couch. It was remarkably cordial given the circumstances. I explained to Ana how utterly horrifying it was that she pulled the trigger, thrice. I explained to Sosa that, although she tried to blast his face off, I am having extraordinary sex with her, and have been otherwise enjoying her company, so I am open to hearing her side of the story. He didn't love that explanation, but he deferred.

"Now," I said, "baby, what's a Gleaner? In this context."

"They're a buncha killers is what they are."

"Chill, Sosa. Let her explain."

"We're just artists, Ray. Like you. Like I said at the bar, we recreate past performances in a contemporary lexicon."

"Ok, let's expound a bit on this *contemporary lexicon*," I said.

"Should be illuminating," Sosa mumbled.

"We're not living in the seventies, you know that, right, Ray? Ask yourself, what would Vito Acconci's body count be if he were born in the new millennium? How could *Following Piece* be realized today without considerable casualties? You've really never heard of us?"

"Of course I have, now that you mention it. I just didn't know you guys gave yourself a name. Kinda poor taste don't you think?"

"Well, it doesn't matter because I've quit. I'm done with performance art. Zombie Formalism is where it's at," said Ana antagonistically.

"Right."

"Why don't you ask your little rent boy here what his story is?" Ana leaned back on the couch triumphantly. She had zero concerns about the attempted murder. "Tell him," she continued. "Who'd you work for before Chattergun?"

"Ray, listen, I've worked for everybody. Literally everybody. Whoever pays, fast. Yeah it was LG who introduced me to Steve Wynn who introduced me to Dmitri Firtash who was a client of Chattergun's. But I've also worked for 'Resistance heroes' (his air quotes) too. I've freelanced for Lisa Cooley, Vito Schnabel, Martha Beck's AI avatar. Shit, my grandfather freelanced for Betty fucking Parsons. I don't have the luxury, Ray, of choosing who pays me."

"I totally get that, dude," I said.

"Of course you do, Ray. You have no spine," observed Ana.

"Listen, Sosa," I said, "everyone's got a right to earn. But if I can't trust you, I can't keep you around."

"Damn, man. You think you can't trust me? For real? I've had your back from jump street, Ray. Who do you think has been keeping Mr. Bridge away? You wanna see the reports I've been submitting?"

"What reports?"

"You sign them every morning, dude. What did you think you were signing?"

"Huh, I don't know." I really didn't know what I thought they were. "Let me see them."

Sosa pulled a manila envelope full of documents from his backpack, which had been left at the foot of the couch. He tried to hand them to me but Ana intercepted them. She paced the room and quickly scanned through the stack of paper.

"Hmm. Not bad. I mean, total bullshit, but not bad." She handed them over to me. I immediately read aloud a random line from the third paragraph.

"A painting isn't just technical expertise in recording what something looks like. A photograph is information, but does not see the same as the eye. Take what you need and leave the rest. A truth, simply told. Core essence. Core value."

"They're notes on your studio practice, Ray, written by you, supposedly," Sosa said. I flipped through another few pages and continued, "I have been investigating the use of camera obscura in studio practice. Pouring over texts by Olafur Eliasson and Lawrence Gowing, who stress indifference to linear convention and extreme economy in modeling. Deep exploration of the Hockney/De Falco Theory..."

"You see, man, I've always had your back. This shit makes you look fucking diligent. When Chattergun finds out it's bullshit, I'll be fired, or worse. Jesus, Ray, I'm desperate for you to make some paintings, and all you do is hang with this psycho girl and binge watch shows. Why don't you try to do some work today?"

He was right, to an extent. "You're wrong, Sosa," I said, "but still, you make some good points. Set up the studio with lighting and a chair. I'm doing a portrait tomorrow."

Later that afternoon, I popped into Chattergun's UES gallery without notice. It's important to be unpredictable. The three-story brownstone was elegant and still smelled of postwar cigars. The receptionist was so surprised when I walked in the door that, when she opened her mouth, she dropped the long end of the thin rubber cord, which was forming a tourniquet around her arm. She was about to plunge a half-bundle's worth of dope into her arm and I spoiled it. She relaxed the rubber cord and the veins in her forearm began to shrink. She was visibly annoyed.

"Mr. Diviner. So nice to see you. You want Nigel? Think he's in a viewing now but I'll check." She picked up the phone. "Yeah, it's him…uh-huh…I know right…ha, as if…" She put the phone down and returned to her fix. Natalie emerged from a large sliding pocket door and beckoned me to follow. We sat in a large private viewing room beneath a Tracy Emin neon that read *"Fuck Off and Die You Slag!"* Natalie handed me a flute of champagne from a table arrangement, which had been quickly set out.

"So, how's it going Ray? I can't tell you how excited we all are to see your new work."

"It's been great. I've never felt so inspired. But that's not why I'm here."

"Oh, should we wait for Mr. Bridge?"

"No, not necessary. It's you who I came to see. You mentioned you have clients interested in commissioning some portraits. I'd like some names. I'm ready to do some sittings, provided the price is right."

"I was hoping you'd say that." She pulled out her phone and sent a text. A minute later an artist liaison entered and handed her a sheet of paper with a list of names. I immediately took it from her. "Oh," I said, "this is interesting. A bit surprising really but…Yeah, I think this could work."

I stopped at Billy Marks, the dive bar on Tenth Ave, and had a few whiskeys as I perused the list of potential sitters. It was an extensive list of the world's biggest collectors, socialites, curators and politicians. I'd choose three. It was all I had time for. After my fourth old fashioned, I settled on David Geffen, Eli Broad and, I couldn't resist, Leo DiCaprio. *Yes*, I thought to myself, *this will do very nicely*. I texted Natalie my choices, and she responded positively. She would make arrangements and schedule sittings for the next few weeks. I work fast, I told her, and I was eager to dive right in. She assured me all three of them were also eager to sit for me, and that there would be museum interest in these portraits when completed. I left the bar feeling drunk and invigorated and made my way downtown to meet Ana at a party for the launch of F Magazine, some fledgling Art & Culture mag.

7

I ARRIVED AT THE PARTY before Ana and chatted jovi-
ally with some old friends. I could feel the eyes of the culture
vultures glued to my back. It was known in these circles that
I had made some major moves and was on the precipice of
stardom. I was chatting with Lynette Yiadom-Boakye, an
old flame of mine, while drinking white wine from a plastic cup, when Ana arrived. She had a laundry bag slung over
her shoulder that looked quite heavy. Being the gentleman
that I am, I offered to carry it for her, but she declined. Ana
scowled at Lynette but, ever graceful and refined, Lynette
did not reciprocate. She kissed me on the cheek, wished me
luck in preparation for my show, and bid me farewell. Ana
was agitated, even more than usual.

"Can we get the fuck out of here? I honestly don't know
why you bother with these people," she said.

"Jesus Christ, baby, if you don't want to be here no one is
forcing you. These are my friends." I was feeling confident
and wasn't particularly receptive to Ana's mood.

"Are they, Ray? Are they your friends? Tell me, when was
the last time you actually spoke to one of these posers? They
don't give a shit about you. Most of them are waiting for you
to fail."

"What the fuck, baby?"

"It doesn't matter. I have other shit to do. You think
you're the only man in my life?"

As she turned to walk away, I noticed an expanding circle

of blood at the bottom of the laundry bag. I reached out and grabbed it. I wasn't ready for the weight, and it plunked to the ground with a thud. Quickly, I pulled the drawstring and peered inside. It was difficult to say for sure, but I think I saw a very large, very dead bird. Ana pulled it from my hands. She was furious.

"A fucking bird?" I exclaimed. "What, are you some kind of ornitho-fucking-ologist now?"

"It's a crane, asshole. A Manchurian Crane. Not easy to come by in New York City. Have fun with your stupid, stuck up, little prick friends. And don't fucking call me."

"Don't worry. I won't."

I spent the rest of the evening getting drunk at the party, talking too much, waxing poetic on the death of the art market, and flirting with undergrad debutantes. I woke up on the couch in my studio with only a foggy memory of how I got home. Sosa entered with the usual racket and tossed a pork chop to Behemoth, still curled up contentedly on his bed in the freight elevator, surrounded by an assortment of chairs.

"I got a call from that cutie at Chattergun. What's her name? Natalie? She told me to pick up a chair for your sitter today. She says you're doing portraits now? That's cool, I guess. It's better than the nothing you've been doing for the past couple of weeks."

Sosa dragged out the chairs one by one and lined them up against the studio wall. "Pick one," he said.

"It depends on who's coming," I said.

Just then the buzzer rang. "Well, let's see, shall we?" Sosa said. I looked into the screen on the intercom and couldn't believe my eyes. David fucking Geffen was at my door. I was not prepared to get right into these portraits. I scrambled to put on some clothes as Sosa buzzed him in. "Don't worry," Sosa assured me, "I've got everything ready."

Mr. Geffen was pleasant, patient, and magnanimous, and he practically assured me he would place the portrait in the LACMA collection upon completion. Sosa had set out a large, leather wingback chair and three stools for his bodyguards. He had already placed a six-foot diameter hexagonal canvas (pre-primed and segmented into 64 areas representing the "eyes") in front of me. It proved a bit difficult to get an unobstructed view through his three bodyguards, but I decided to incorporate the guards into the portrait. After all, were they not part of the essence of the man? I sketched out the important elements quickly, with short, erratic gestures. I repeated the curve of his sleek, bald head in the upper segments, his wide-set eyes beneath two thick, black brows in others. His mouth changed as he spoke, and I tried to capture its fluctuations between small talk and chit-chat. I suppressed the desire to pepper him with questions about his past, about the musicians whose careers he cultivated, and instead worked feverishly on nailing down the crux of his spirit. My pencil glided along the canvas effortlessly, and I dared not lose my focus. When I was finished, he left, showing no interest in viewing my rendering of him, which I respected greatly. I interpreted it as faith in me as an artist, rather than the more probable disinterest. The next week was spent finishing this work in oil paint, which I was able to accomplish peacefully and diligently, with no distraction from Ana.

I had not heard from her since the fight and I did not miss her. It felt great to engage with my work in a way I had been unable to in the midst of our romantic chaos. Sosa was thrilled to have her out of his hair. He kept reminding me of this, of how much trouble she had been causing us, in the form of newspaper clippings that referenced bloody performances staged by the Gleaners. Articles with headlines like "Mayhem in GagWater Lobby" or "Christie's Auction Disrupted by Shootout" were left on the coffee table at my studio. There was no doubt in my mind that she and her crew were behind these events. Good riddance to bad rubbish, I say.

My next sitter was Eli Broad. I had read his book, *The Art of Being Unreasonable*, while attending an artist residency last summer, and it left a strong impression on me. His words resonated deeply with my younger self. "All progress depends on the unreasonable man," he states, and he was not wrong. My formative years were spent fighting against my naturally reasonable nature. In retrospect it may have done more harm than good, but it's impossible to say for sure. Being unreasonable is a privilege, I think, one that requires a significant safety net, which I've never had. During our portrait session however, I found him to be temperate, sensible and very reasonable. So reasonable, in fact, that he barely said a word to me the entire time, and we were able to complete the sitting in a little over three hours.

The portrait session for my next sitter turned out to be quite the opposite. Mr. DiCaprio arrived six hours late and with an entourage consisting of two bodyguards, three fashion models, a stylist, his agent, a spiritual advisor and Jonah Hill. They showed very little interest in actually getting the portrait finished. Instead, we spent our time together doing coke and drinking champagne and vodka. There was a little fucking and lots of laughter interspersed with some exceptionally in-depth discussions about art theory and the art market. Leo really surprised me with his insights. For instance, when I wondered aloud what would be the ultimate home for this particular portrait, a museum or private collection, Leonardo astutely quoted Richard Wollheim and proclaimed, "A painter makes paintings, but it takes a representative of the art world to make a work of art." The fact that he said this while doing a line of coke off of the thigh of a six-foot Bulgarian fashion model made it that much more impressive. He inquired about my feelings on Rosalind Krauss's theory that the avant-garde should be conceived as a literal origin rather than a dissolution of the past, and I clumsily answered that I agreed. They left my studio just before midnight. I finished my portrait via photographs and movie stills. Later, I used this as an excuse to rewatch some of my favorites of his films: *The Basketball Diaries*, *Gilbert Grape*, and the *Titanic* trilogy. (Yes, if you're wondering, I had to restrain myself from saying I'd "paint him like one of his French girls.")

A few days later the gallery sent over a crew of art handlers to pack and transport the new portraits. The local art transport company, which runs the neighborhoods of Gowanus, Redhook and South Slope, is called Maquette FAS. They are a rough crew, known to be fanatical in their work and not to be trifled with. Sosa made sure to answer the door with a revolver tucked visibly into his belt. Many of the art handling services work as agents for unscrupulous dealers and advisors, so I kept a close eye on them as they worked. When I insisted the works be shadowboxed, as some of the oil paint was not fully dry, they hesitated but eventually relented. Once they were finished, they loaded the works in the freight elevator, and I decided to take a well deserved rest. Nigel had offered me use of his vacation home in Amagansett, Long Island, and I took the Jitney up for a long weekend.

8

THE HAMPTONS WERE empty this time of year. Most of the restaurants were closed, which suited me just fine, as I had little interest in dining out anyway. It also meant the usual traffic from wealthy city folk on weekend getaways was virtually nonexistent. Nigel owned a sprawling estate on the waterfront overlooking Napeague Bay. I woke early on Saturday morning and took a long walk along the beach. It dawned on me then that I hadn't actually been alone in quite a long time, and it made me a bit uncomfortable. Solitude raises the voices of my inner demons above their usual whispers. I find more peace in the cacophonous racket of city life than in the silent focus of the countryside. I need the booming thump of garbage trucks, the pounding repetition of construction, the rumbling pulse of the cosmopolites to keep my mind-goblins at bay. The hollow wind whistling through my ears, interspersed only by the repetitive lapping of the waves on the shore, brought attention to my every mental shortcoming and began to crush me with self-doubt.

"Your exhibition is weak and derivative."

"You haven't had an original idea since grad school."

"No one will ever love you for yourself. You will never love someone for noble reasons. You are purely driven by sex."

"You've coasted by on good looks most of your life. But you're not even that good looking."

"You have an exhibition space to fill, but you're an empty fucking shell."

I was reminded of a conversation I once had, in 2007 with Helene Winer at Angelika Film Center, sipping espresso at the New York premier of *Paris je t'aime*, discussing her theory on gallery ownership as a performative experience. She believed that exhibiting artwork is at its core an anthropomorphic interpretation of space as a physical body, walls as skin, studs as bones, foundation as spine and artwork as the DNA, animating the otherwise lifeless framework. Gallery owner as *architect*, she said, in the ancient Greek theater connotation of the word, as someone who leads others into action. I reminded her of the inescapable labyrinth Daedalus built, and that perhaps his analogy was flawed, but no, she said, that is entirely the point. Her theory seemed like a stretch to me at the time, but now I see its truth.

I woke up on the couch in the early evening hung over and in a pitiful state. The television screen had paused and posed an existential question from Netflix, "Are you still there?"

I spent the rest of the evening smoking joints, dancing around the living room listening to Caetano Veloso, with *Microcosmos* playing on mute on the large flat screen TV. It was the best time I'd had in months. In the morning I called an Uber to the bus station, cutting my weekend short, eager to get back to the babble of the city and the introspective amnesia it brings.

9

I TOOK THE FREIGHT elevator up to my studio. Behemoth was sound asleep on the elevator floor in what had become a quasi-luxury flat for the dog, and I was happy for him. However, when the large elevator doors slid open, I found Sosa furiously tearing the place apart.

"What the fuck, dude? Have you lost your mind?"

He was balanced on top of a stool running his hand along the ceiling beams, searching for something. He kept searching frantically as he spoke.

"Everything's fucked, man," he said. "She's screwed us big time. You probably shouldn't be here."

"What do you mean?"

"Don't you check the news? Look at Twitter. See who's trending."

Oh my god. A quick glance at my phone, and I immediately knew what he was referring to. All three of my sitters, Eli Broad, David Geffen, and Leo DiCaprio had gone missing, possibly killed. This was bad. Sosa was right; it had to be her. If not exactly her, definitely the Gleaners. Sosa hopped down from the stool and ran over to the kitchen table where a pile of surveillance gear lay in the middle.

"She'd been watching the whole time. Plotting this shit. She's framing you, dude."

"No way. I mean, just no way."

I don't know why I trusted her but I did. *God damn it, Ray*, I thought to myself, *you're so fucking stupid*. I walked over to the couch and collapsed. The room spun around me. I searched my brain for clues I may have missed but couldn't find any. Obviously I knew she was capable of doing this, but I never thought she would do it *to me*. Fucking pride I guess. I should've known I wasn't special to her. Just then the buzzer to the studio rang and my heart sunk. I assumed it was the cops and was only slightly relieved to see Nigel and Natalie in the intercom. When Sosa opened the door, they barged right through and stood over me as I shrunk in shame between the couch cushions.

"We're opening, Ray," said Natalie, "tomorrow evening. The VIP event starts at 6:00."

"I'm...I'm...not ready."

"But *we* are, boy," said Nigel, "and the show opens tomorrow. It's been installed. The press preview is today. You don't need to be there."

"I'd like to be there."

"It's best if you just lay low, Ray. With all the police activity surrounding your exhibition...We'd like things to not escalate any further than they already have," Natalie said.

"And clean this shithole up, mate. You'll need to be out of here by the end of the week," said Nigel.

10

TODAY IS THE DAY. I am done writing down my story. I hope it illuminates my experience and perspective. I have a killer headache, most likely from stress. It is already half past noon, and Sosa is nowhere to be found. Part of me thinks I'll never see him again. I turn on the TV and watch the news. I search the Internet for any updates on the missing persons but nothing comes up. I try to call Ana but her phone is deactivated. I call Chattergun, but I am told by the receptionist that Nigel and Natalie are not available. This doesn't feel right, and honestly I'm getting frightened. I knew they were dangerous people when I got involved with them. It's like making a deal with a Mafia family, or some Faustian bargain, but my ambition drove me on. I find myself whispering words from Pacino's character in the grossly underrated 1997 film *Devil's Advocate*, "Vanity, definitely my favorite sin."

I sit on the couch for an hour, maybe more, staring at a blue screen on the television. The cable must've gone out but I don't notice. I keep replaying scenes from the last few months in my mind, correcting myself, making different choices, creating alternate realities, but nothing changes the fact that I am here, that I am me, and that I am terrified of the coming evening.

I hear my phone ping, and I see I have six messages, all from Natalie. They planned for a livery car to pick me up in…*shit*…eight minutes. I rifle through my closet in a frenzy but then I stop myself. Surely I can't show up in this state,

lacking confidence, lacking swagger. Tonight is too important for me to be hesitant. I step back and turn to the mirror.
Fine. Just fine. But I am missing a key element. I step over to
my work area and pick up a plastic cup half filled with white
acrylic paint. I lean my head back. Far back. I hold the cup
above my head and tilt it. A stream of paint hits my forehead
and I feel invigorated. It is cold as it runs down my nose,
around my nostril and into my lips. I'm revitalized. I let it
dry like mud from a river bed. Like a baptism. I feel something divine. Ray motherfucking Diviner.

I throw on my hoodie and overcoat and step into the
open freight elevator. Behemoth, along with his multitude
of accumulated belongings, is no longer there. The livery
cab takes me through the Battery Tunnel and up the Westside Highway into Chelsea.

I tell the driver to let me off a few blocks away, and I walk
towards 24th Street. The crowds are thick on the Chelsea
sidewalks, which is not uncommon for a Thursday evening,
when galleries are all holding opening receptions for their
new exhibitions. The crowd on 24th is thicker than most,
and when I turn the corner I see why. Chattergun Gallery
is located in the middle of the block, flanked by buildings
on both sides. Well, previously flanked by buildings on both
sides. Now it stands alone. The rubble from the other galleries still litters the ground, but Chattergun is like a solitary
cathedral, like a church spared from the carpet bombs of
WW2. I see pairs of circular stained glass windows installed
high along the sides of the gallery. Catherine windows, like
the Rose of Strasburg or Notre Dame, but instead of holy
quatrefoils, I see a tracery of hexagons radiating from a central roundel. My god, they are my eyes, my Fly-Eyes.

I push through the crowd and see a larger, more gothic
rose window in the façade of the gallery. The well-dressed
crowd of art stars and socialites recognize me and form a
path for me. I push past the security guards and enter. It is

absolutely stunning. The gallery is darkened so that light outside pours in solely through the large, colorful oculi and projects the Fly-Eyes on the walls. It is absolutely heavenly. It is perfect. It is transcendent, truly, but it is not mine. I spin around the room in confusion and awe. I can't take my eyes off the godlike projections. I hear a single clap, followed by another, then joined by more. Turning around I see the man, James Chattergun, offering me slow applause and taking a step forward. He approaches me, and I feel weak. He puts both hands on my shoulders and looks me square in the eyes. His Dior suit is perfectly pressed but his teeth are rotten.

"Well done, boy," he says.

"I didn't…This isn't…"

"Then who did, eh? Of course you did. This is the show you were born to make, boy."

The doors open and the gallery floods with spectators. In a minute, it is full. They give me space, forming a circle around me, as if I were a holy man, untouchable. There must be two hundred people in the gallery; clients, critics, fans, but no one makes a sound. Natalie breaks the circle and hands me a flute of champagne. I take a sip. I smile.

11

TESS DIVINER
New York, 1987

TESS DIVINER HELD HER newborn baby boy close to her chest as she slunk off of the inbound train at Grand Central Station. She kept her eyes on her feet and counted the flat black spots of chewing gum on the concrete platform as she walked towards the exit. She took the escalator up to street level, hailed a taxi and directed the driver to 40 Mercer Street, the apartment of her ex-boyfriend, Nigel. She wasn't exactly sure what she wanted from him. She had told him she wasn't going to keep the child, and she really hadn't planned to. She didn't need money, and she didn't want it. She hadn't given the boy a name because that is a father's job, she believed, wrongly. But she just thought that he, Nigel, should be given the opportunity to love the child, and if he didn't want to, then so be it. He most likely would not care, but at least she would know, and they would be back to Grand Central, then home to Connecticut. She rang the buzzer to his converted loft and waited. Her child looked at her with concerned blue eyes but did not cry.

Twenty minutes earlier, Nigel had been visited by his boss, friend, and fellow up-and-coming art world star James Chattergun. James was quite agitated when he burst through the door.

"Tell me it's done, Nige. We can't afford any fuck-ups," he said.

"Nothing to worry about, Captain. I've taxed the boiler beyond its capacity and it'll blow any minute now. I hired a crew to adjust it yesterday, and we can easily lay the blame on them. I've checked our insurance policies and we are maxed out and up to date."

"Great. No mistakes this time. Who the fuck is that?"

The buzzer to his loft groaned like a crushed toddler and startled both of the men. Nigel sprung to his feet and checked the monitor, which hung to the left of the stainless steel doorframe. He could not distinguish the figure outside on the blurry, black and white video screen. It wasn't until she lifted her eyes, full of distress and anticipation, that Nigel was able to identify the misty figure as the former intern at the gallery, Tess Diviner. "Fuck me," he said, upon seeing the oblong bundle in her arms. He didn't have any clear memory of having a romance with her, but his cock stiffened a little when he saw her blurred but sanguine eyes. He was seconds away from pressing the intercom and cursing her out when James stopped him.

"Don't answer. Let her go, man. Unless you want to be a daddy, eh?"

"Might not be mine, Boss. You remember the sales retreat last spring. Could be anybody's."

"Well, just ignore her then. We've got business tonight."

She stood by the door for fifteen minutes. Five of those minutes were spent in hopeful ideation. Seven were spent in unease and fright. Her mindset during the remaining three minutes cannot be described with any traditional literary contrivance. She wandered around SoHo for a while, stopping to peer in the window at the Liza Lou exhibition at Deitch-Halliburton Projects, then made her way back to Chattergun Fine Arts on Greene Street.

The gallery's windows were smashed and the door was

ajar. Almost no one else would have entered, due to the overwhelming smell of propane that filled the exhibition space. Tess Diviner, however, had inherited a condition known as Congenital Anosmia, which left her without olfactory senses. She slipped through the small opening in the large doors, and past a black sign on the large white wall, which read "Surrealist Masters In Love." Her heart was filled with a sense of heroic steadfastness. Nothing but moonlight fell on the prewar masterpieces lining the wall.

"Nigel!"

She cried out his name as she scurried past Max Ernst's *Bird and Dove*, 1927, casting her shadow against the soaring, jagged structures on the thin canvas. She stumbled a bit and slid across Victor Brauner's *Fascination*, 1939, leaving a horizontal scuff on the anthropomorphized tabletop. It wasn't long until the effects of the gas overcame her. Her vision blurred and her knees buckled. "*Nigel*," she whispered, as she fell into an easel and tumbled unconscious to the floor, her baby tucked tightly in her arms, causing Man Ray's *Observatory Time – The Lovers*, 1932 to topple onto them. As if choreographed by a divine playwright, a burst of flame shot through the gallery from the boiler room, singeing everything in its path, save for the mother and child flattened on the stone floor beneath the large Surrealist canvas.

Within moments, FDNY Ladder 25 was on the scene. Torrents of water were shot from the heavy hoses. The gas line was remotely shut off and the fire soon extinguished. The gallery filled with men in burdensome rubber suits. The paintings were black and waterlogged, and smoke drifted from their stretcher bars in ghostly wisps. Tess Diviner made a little noise when she exhaled her last breath, but the firemen did not hear it above the crackle of embers and the sirens wailing outside. The little boy heard it (as he sometimes still does, right before waking from unsettling dreams, sweaty and gasping for air). He started crying and that is what the firemen heard.

"Over here!" cried a man who looked just like Kurt Russell's character from *Backdraft*.

"Fuck! Is that a fucking baby?" shouted another man who totally resembled Steve McQueen's character from *The Towering Inferno*.

Robert Urich's character from *Turk 182* flipped the canvas over and scooped the boy up in his arms. "It's ok, little guy." The little guy cried.

"Look at that," Kurt Russell said. "Man Ray, *Observatory Time – The Lovers*, 1932. You know, this is just one of many paintings inspired by his lover, Kiki De Montparnasse. These are her lips painted across the sky, even."

"No, you stupid fucking idiot. These are Lee Miller's lips painted across the sky, even," said Robert Urich as he turned and walked away with the child cradled in his arms. "Let's get that body out of here."

The Gleaners

1

TODAY WAS DISGUSTING. Not unlike yesterday, but today had a supremely fucking elevated vulgarity. Like pulverized livestock dripping with shit and sex. Disgusting stuff. Think Carolee Schneemann's *Meat Joy* performed in the jungles during the 1965 Siege of Plei Me, or behind the hanging blue tarps at The Cock on Avenue A.

A better man might be bothered by it all, and almost anybody is a better man than me, so fuck it. Cunt them all. Kick their muffs in. Smash their dicks into their throats.

Hi, I'm Darren. I'm driving around and listening to some tunes. I stink of cow intestines, fat and garbage and I'm covered in blood.

Sometimes I feel so horny!
Sometimes I feel so mad!
Sometimes I feel so horny!
But mostly I suck on gonads!

Linger on! My pale blue balls!
Linger ooooon! My pale blue balls!

I fucking love Lou Reed, but fuck him, right? That's what love is, right? Repeating death, over, over, over again, in bite-sized chunks of fuck, fuck, fuck again. Giving a little afterlife to the only thing that means anything to you. Right? Six-inch death stab. Dig your death-prick into a warm cunt-grave and fuck the only thing you give a shit about. Yeah, that's right. Oooh baby, that's right. Right there. Harder. Faster. Make art. Make cum. Make art cum. I love art. I love to see it. Naked on a gallery wall. To create it. But(t) fuck art. Right?

Today marks the six-month anniversary of a game-changing performance we staged in the GagWater lobby. Me and the other Gleaners had been planning it for weeks. At the time, they had two large Ed Ruscha works flanking the marble entrance to their Madison Ave location, and I was eager to perform a fiendish *Motif In Light*. The other members of my performance group all had their own ideas of what this performance should be, which caused quite a bit of contention during the planning process, and ultimately proved to be the first crack in the unity of our little troupe.

The Gleaners have five primary members. We all have our distinctions and idiosyncrasies, and we are all stone cold motherfuckers. Who's up?

Jayme H. Christ, our youngest performer at 22, loves all things Arte Povera, particularly the anarchic freedom of Jannis Kounellis. He was a feared and successful art handler before finding his true calling as a Resistance artist. His skill at planting listening devices brought him to the attention of the Resistance, where he successfully planted bugs in the offices or residences of Amy Cappalazzo, Julian Schnabel, Thelma Golden, Marc Payot and Emmanuel Perrotin. On his last day working as an art handler, Jayme set fire to a 17-foot box truck carrying the entirety of a David Zwirner Lisa Yuskavage show and rode the top like a surfboard as it crashed into the brick wall surrounding the old seminary on Tenth Ave. His brother, Andy, who was driving the vehicle, is still locked up in the seminary's on-site prison.

Josephine Bonaparte, 27, is a total stan of Marina Abromović. Her recreation of *Balkan Baroque* using the bones of the cast of *The View* is credited with ending the years long "Fake News Siege." She emigrated from Haiti in the aftermath of the 2010 hurricane and settled in New Jersey. The only record of her existence comes from a restraining order against her by Treach (from Naughty By Nature) in 2012. Otherwise, she is a ghost. She once told me a story, after a long night of champagne, molly and blow, about her work as a model for a series of XXX-rated paintings by Wilson Bigaud, which were commissioned by then-President Jean-Bertrand Aristide. In the paintings, Josephine, barely a teen at the time, poses in vividly obscene tableaus involving look-alikes of Bill and Hillary Clinton and other administration officials, most notably Zoe Baird and Kimba Wood. The US media whitewashed the discovery of these paintings as "Nannygate," but the fallout is widely believed to have been the root cause of the CIA backed paramilitary coup that sent President Aristide into exile. Not only do I believe the story is true, I also believe Josephine left out some of the more scandalous details.

Jimmy Kanter, our sole quadragenarian member, is old school, into Cabaret Voltaire, not particularly concerned with conceptual purism as long as there was nihilism, disorder and an opportunity to howl Huelsenbeck poems drunkenly through a megaphone. Jimmy had become quite famous as a commander of a Blackwater Tactical Support Team, and was known for his deep love of art and brutality. In 2011, viral videos appeared of him dragging Gaddafi's mangled corpse down Al Jamahiriya Street chanting a famous quote from Tristan Tzara, "Dance, dance my beautiful insouciance! The world burns and you laugh, with forced laughter." The videos were ultimately used as evidence of Blackwater's involvement in the Arab Spring uprisings. After a dishonorable discharge from Blackwater, he reportedly stayed in Tripoli for years after the coup, living in the subterranean rubble of the old Finance Ministry, and founding a community of performers based around the tenets of the Dada Manifesto.

Ana is obsessed with maintaining (or even upping the

ante of) the conceptual spirit in the performances she recreates. It drives me crazy. She is excessively violent (which is perhaps her most charming feature besides her tits and ass), and has taken to solely recreating La Monte Young performance scores. She alone has given me more pain than all of the collected betrayals, disappointments, beatings and big-time-ass-kickings of my 33-year life rolled up together like a fist and rocketed into my face.

We ultimately decided this particular performance in the GagWater lobby would be a democratic menagerie of our personal predilections. A big mistake, it turns out, because the lack of a clearly articulated artistic focus would lead us down a fatal road of missteps, jealousy, violence and heartache.

2

THE GLEANERS ARE SLICK, you see? We are always dressed to the nines. Not because we are wealthy (far from it) but because we have a calculated tendency to seek out and attack professional art advisors (primarily, although collectors and salespeople garner a fair amount of our attention). We stalk them, drug them, fuck them whenever possible, and always leave with part or all of their very expensive wardrobes. Just the other week, Josephine brought us a luggage case filled with Hugo Boss suits that she took from the yacht of an advisor from Art Agency. We share our clothes and we share our beds, and both the sex and threads are top-notch.

The performance at the GagWater lobby was fated to be the moment when Ana met (and potentially fell in love with, but who knows with her) that son of a bitch salesman from GagWater. That was the first day I ever doubted her ability to be our leader, if that's what she is. After that, her performances became more frequent, sloppy and deadly, ultimately culminating in what is now called *The Red Auction* when she shot that bastard Bespoke Downs. Her final betrayal of that fucker Downs was largely seen by the other Gleaners as being an affirmation of her status as leader of the troupe, but not by me. I only saw weakness. Much like a banal, final act in a tired Tennessee Williams play, she's become predictable and dull. If it was a strategy, then it was botched and ineffective. If it was love, then it was a petty bourgeois luxury. Either way, she quickly regained her footing by kidnapping three of the most high-profile art collectors through her manipulation of that other fool, Ray Diviner. She played that poor fucker like a fiddle. It truly was a master class on emotional exploitation. That boy is mostly ego. Easy to toy with. The dumb fuck doesn't even know who his daddy is, even though everyone else in the art world does. Secret fucking trust fund and the boy who would be king. The boy with the big gallery show. Opens tonight. His coronation. The day has already been long, and, as mentioned, quite disgusting, but the night is jailbait, and there is much work to do.

Let me walk you guys through it. Starting from the break of dawn.

The white light from the midwinter sunrise had yet to lick the large stone faces of the brownstones along Malcolm X Blvd. I was already up, dressed, and downing my third cup of coffee before the sun rose. I was probably still drunk from last night, but I was dead set on the day's objective. You see, the Gleaners had planned a performance for the afterparty of Diviner's Chattergun show. We planned on recreating some of Hermann Nitsch's *Orgien Mysterien Theater* with our three prized prisoners. We'd subject Mr. Geffen, Mr. Broad and Mr. DiCaprio to an onslaught of sensory theater designed to reduce the mechanisms of its analysis to a purely material experience. *Music to noise. Language to scream. And spilling paint to opened entrails.* Our plan was to film the recreation of the performance, then have the film projected onto the walls of Bagatelle during the afterparty. Each projection was manipulated to be in the shape of large, hexagonal "Fly-Eyes." It is a great plan.

We've only just wrapped up the first part, filming the performance with our three guests, and I am completely drenched in the byproducts of its essential elements. Blood, pork fat, sex, wine, saliva, you name it. The stains on my white lab coat could also serve as a "pure painting" to potentially be included in a future exhibition (fingers crossed). The brutal celebration reached its orgiastic climax in a mix of crimson blood and the soft organs of livestock, accompanied by an assortment of hand drums, shouts and brass instruments, which provided a pulsating crescendo. Mr. Geffen was the first to reach catharsis, followed by Mr. DiCaprio then Mr. Broad. I really don't give a fuck, but it does make for riveting viewing.

The other Gleaners are getting in position at the restaurant, securing the ceiling mounts for the projectors, syncing up the footage, cueing the soundtrack (we decided on a live version of "I'm Sticking With You" where Moe Tucker's vocals are particularly child-like and pure). I imagine Ray Diviner is currently basking in the glow of his glorious installation, pressing the flesh with collectors and high-ranking government officials, completely oblivious to the perils of his immediate future.

You see, Ana's plan was to ambush Diviner and the Chattergun crew while they were feeling relaxed in the triumphant air of the afterparty. After a presumably explosive entrance, she would "secure" the guests of honor and begin the viewing of our previously recorded version of Nitsch's "action."

I, however, have other plans.

I imagine Ana waiting, perched in some dark corner or possibly posing as a hostess, growing restless and impatient, as she waits for the Diviner party to arrive. But the party won't arrive.

Hear that? That banging? That's Ray Diviner, in the trunk of my car.

I turn up the volume on my "VU Essentials" playlist to cover the cacophony coming from the interior storage of my sedan.

Some people fuck very hard!
But still they never do it right!
Oh baby I'm beginning to see the light!

My plan is to spoon out his eyes and replace them with snow globes stolen from the MoMA gift shop. Imagine a plastic Frida Kahlo and *The Scream* swirling with glitter, jammed into his empty eye sockets. Pretty good, right? Maybe I'll leave him in Ana's apartment so that when she comes home, late, having run the whole gauntlet of failure and disappointment, she'll open the door to find him hog-tied on the floor. And then she'll break.

But first, I have a stop to make. I'll need a hand with all of this and I know just the man.

3

I PARK MY SAAB 9000 on 58th Street and grab a can of
WD-40 and my phone. I discreetly make my way down Park
to 57th and ascend the marble stairs of the Consulate General to the Republic of Korea. There is no one at the reception desk, no guard, but when I press the call button for the
elevator, I swear I hear someone moaning from behind the
wraparound desk. I don't take it to the top floor. I get off
one below and creep up the stairs. Stealth like. A fucking
puma. I'm looking for someone. Can you guess who?

I spray the lubricant I brought on the hinges on the door
to the top floor stairwell. It drips down the hinge and the
doorframe, and I let it soak a bit before spraying some more.
Smells so good. Like petrichor. The door opens noiselessly
and I see him by the window, seated in his wheelchair with
the scope of a sniper rifle pressed to his eye. His designer suit. The vintage Nikes. The stupid fucking makeup
smeared across his nose. I crawl across the floor slowly, like
a slug, and slide my body under a bench in what appears to
be a waiting room. The window offers a perfect view across
57th Street, specifically to the private viewing rooms of Phillips Auction House.

The brightly lit rooms of the auction house make for
brightly lit targets. The unfortunate attempt by Markus
Dochantschi to create an inclusive and innervated vibe
in the auction house ultimately created a sleek, perfectly
framed death trap. I squint my eyes and see a finely dressed

woman in front of Barnett Newman's *Onement V,* 1948 gesturing to a well-dressed man, all behind a large, crystal-clean glass window. She is pointing out a minor condition issue, and he leans forward so that his eyes are an inch from the center of the painting. His head is perfectly bifurcated by a vertical green painted line.

I glance back at the man in the wheelchair. I admire his steady hand on the sniper rifle, his aim so tight it'd squeeze the jizz from a dust mite's scrotum. Damn that bastard looks sharp. I hate the motherfucker, but enlisting him in my plan may just be my magnum opus. I see him draw a deep breath and hold it, moments away from pulling the trigger. I lean out from under the bench and rest my chin in my hands and look at him adoringly.

"Yo! Downs!"

"Motherfuck," he says. "Can't this wait a minute? The sublime is now, you know."

I roll myself out completely and brush myself off as I stand, even though I'm still wearing the white lab coat and even though it's covered in dried blood and guts. He looks me up and down without moving the rifle from its ready position.

"Love the coat," he says, "what is it? Alexander McQueen?"

"I got something you're gonna wanna see, Downs."

"Please, it's Bespoke. Beeee-spoke. But do give me a minute to finish my painting."

"Sure, of course," I say.

He returns his eye to the scope of the sniper rifle and takes another breath. He holds it, whispers, "*The sublime… is…now,*" and squeezes the trigger, sending a high-velocity round out of the top floor window of the Consulate General to the Republic of Korea, across 57th Street, through the large glass window of the Phillips Auction House viewing room, in and out of the head of the finely dressed man examining the painting, and into the center of Barnett Newman's *Onement V,* 1948. The man jolts forward and slides across the painting, leaving a smear of blood across its "zip."

Bespoke lowers the gun and leans his head out of the window for a better look. I hear the woman scream from across the street, and it echoes around the thoroughfare.

"Not bad. Not bad at all."

He spins his wheelchair towards me and moves into the light. I am finally face to face with a man who I have spent the last six months hating. He is handsome, but he now lacks the swagger that brought him fame. Being partially paralyzed from the waist down will do that to a man. He begins dismantling his sniper rifle and packing it in a suitcase.

"You were saying? Something I'd want to see?"

"Yeah. A mutual friend. Well, a mutual interest. He's in the trunk of my car."

"Color me intrigued. Help me out here, brother."

As I walk around him I glance out the window and get a good look at the large Newman painting with the blood streaked across its face. A smile creeps upon mine. I grab the handles on his wheelchair and push him towards the elevator.

"*Altered Masterpieces.* That's what I call them. I'm an artist now. This is my thing, my series," says the former art advisor turned artist, Bespoke Downs.

The elevator doors open and we enter. Bespoke presses the "B - Staff Only" button at the bottom of the panel. The doors slide closed without a sound. I introduce myself.

"I'm Darren Dingman," I say, truthfully. "I believe you know my wife."

"Your wife? Oh. Ha. Your wife. Of course. 'Hi, I'm Ana,' she says. Ha, of course, your wife…"

"That's her."

"Nice to meet you, Mr. Dyingman," Bespoke says mockingly. "You know, Robert Irwin once noted that if you hold up a red square in front of you, on a sunny day, then take it away, your eye will see a green square. It's how eyes work. Now imagine the same phenomena taking place in your heart. If the red square is love, then when it goes away, what's the green square? Ana is a red square, Darren, but tell me, what's the green square?"

The elevators open, and I wheel him across an empty parking garage then up a ramp and onto Fifth Ave. I park him behind my Saab and pop the trunk. Bespoke leans in.

"Oh wow. That's Ray Diviner. Chattergun's new great white hope."

"Sure is."

"What are you going to do with him?"

"I'm going to gouge out his eyes, I think."

"No. That won't do. Not both eyes. Just the one. Dim the lights a bit."

The man in my trunk moans but does not wake. I slam the trunk hatch shut. I help Bespoke into the passenger side and stow his wheelchair in the back seat. He asks for his briefcase and I give it to him. As we drive away he begins reassembling his sniper rifle. "It's all I got on me," he explains, most likely a lie.

We take the Westside Highway and head south. The radio plays NPR and Terry Gross is interviewing Larry Gagosian. He is explaining to her that despite the abduction of two of his best selling artists, John Currin and Dan Colen, his new Mexico City location is still profitable due to the insurance policies he astutely took out. Ms. Gross is nonplussed.

"You know," says Bespoke, "when I worked for GagWater, he took out K&R policies on all of his artists, and on some of his salespeople."

"K&R?" I ask.

"Kidnap and Ransom. He's such a crafty business man."

"Yeah, he's a legend."

We hear some pounding coming from the trunk. Our art star has come to. *Just as well*, I think, *we need to walk from here.* I exit at 14th Street and park on Eighth Ave. I lift Downs into his wheelchair and pop the trunk. The look in Diviner's eyes is dazed, but undeniably filled with sheer terror. "Good day, sunshine," I say. Bespoke pulls a small syringe out from his wrist bandana. "May I?"

"Go for it," I say.

Bespoke gleefully jabs Diviner in the arm, causing his eyes to pop open as he springs upright.

"You. I know you. You're Ana's friend. From the bar uptown," Diviner says.

"Ana's husband," I correct him.

"What the fuck is going on?"

I pull out the revolver that I'd tucked in my belt and point it at him.

"You're gonna have a bad day, Ray. Get out. Now. Get the fuck out!"

I grab him by the ear and pull him violently to his feet. He screams but complies. "Bitch," I say.

"Where to now, friends?" Bespoke inquires.

"The only way to get where we need to go. Down," I say.

4

WE TAKE THE ELEVATOR down to L'exchange market. The only handicap accessible entrance with even a minimal chance of survival is at Eighth Ave. The underground market gets increasingly dangerous as you move east towards Brooklyn. The interior of the elevator is a shitty mock-up of a Kusama Infinity Room, with bulbs of light reflecting off of an inch-deep puddle of urine on the diamond plated steel floor. Ray Diviner is behind Bespoke Downs, pushing his chair, as I stand next to them, revolver in hand, silently laughing my ass off. Diviner is scared and submissive. Downs is downright giddy. The doors slide open, and we step out into the nihilistic marketplace.

The western end of the market is reminiscent of Times Square in the late seventies, or like the Bolivian La Paz market (if Bolivians were sadomasochistic mercenaries), and it's quite lovely. The marketplace begins with a rather high-end sex trade, progresses to narcotics near Union Square, contraband by First Ave and, by the time you get to Brooklyn (assuming you survive the 1.5 mile tunnel under the East River), the market opens up to all sorts of illicit wares. I've never actually made it past the Morgan stop, which is best described as a GG Allin concert where all of the audience members are also GG Allin. The Gleaners headquarters are in a ramshackle niche near the G train at Metropolitan Ave, part of an enclave of Resistance troupes known as The New Met Opera. I am taking my trio there to unveil my master-plan when the rest of the Gleaners return. It is just after midnight, and I imagine they'll return around 1 or 2 a.m., dejected and disconsolate.

The whores at this end of the tunnel are fucking marvelous. So hot I can feel my dick jump and twitch inside my jeans. Tits bulging from tight Lycra, ass cheeks exposed and enticing, heavily perfumed, with hoop earrings. Fuck me. I want them all. They smile and beckon and I smile back and Bespoke nonchalantly rubs his cock and Ray Diviner does nothing at all. The pimps in this area are minor celebrities in their own right. In fact, quite a few celebrities have taken on a second career here as pimps. Jarvis Cocker, Steve Buscemi, Colin Firth and Sting each have their own stable of top notch rent-a-puss. But even they don't have the popularity, stardom even, of the homegrown pimps of L'exchange. Friday nights turn this stretch of the tunnel into the most happening place in the city. Wall Street types mix with politicians and gangsters while perusing the virtues of transsexual sex dolls. Nobody bats an eye at the revolver I am pointing at Ray Diviner's head (quite the opposite in fact, as one of the more famous prostitutes here, a waiflike them known as Le Kate Moss, smiles and says, "Wanna use that shooter on me, sweetie?").

I waste no time on small talk with the girls and urge Bespoke to focus on our business. The odor of perfume from the undoubtedly infected prostitutes gives way to the thick stench of pot smoke and freebasing as we near Union Square. Shouts of "Three for ten!" and "High octane!" bounce off of the tiled walls.

"Hold up," Bespoke says, "let's get lit, eh?"

I shrug and Diviner shrugs and almost instantly Bespoke is handed a blunt by one of the many dealers lining the tunnel.

"Waddup, Downs?" the dealer says as he and Bespoke bump fists casually. We walk and smoke. Diviner gets surprisingly chatty when high.

"Art, like drugs, is a low-level search for god," he says.

"Oh this is fun," says Downs. "Art, like wine, has a mercurial essence which makes its quality subject to an individual's dubious taste. You try, Darren!"

"Art, like the promises of a woman, should be painted on running water."

The three of us laugh and pass the dutchie to the left hand side.

"So, you guys are definitely gonna kill me, eh?" Ray says, snuffing out the vibe.

"Well, definitely gonna blind you," I reply.

"Definitely going to partially blind you," Bespoke corrects me.

"Nothing I can do to change your minds?"

"You've made your bed, Ray, and you know it."

"By falling in love with the same woman you bastards also fell in love with?"

"Yes, but also by shamelessly monetizing your work. You see, strategy is a commodity, but execution is an art. We execute people like you, as an art, with very little strategy. It's quite simple really."

"Do you suppose I'm unaware of my guilt? Existing to enrich the lives of the privileged elite is hardly what drew me to a life as an artist."

"Well then, Ray Diviner," Downs mocks, "what was it then. Was it love? Of art? Of women? Of a woman?"

"Fuck you, man," Ray sneers back. "Yeah, maybe I loved her and maybe I just loved fucking her but you know what? You sorry ass motherfuckers did the same. Downs, we've all been laughing our asses off talking about your cripple ass. Just tonight, Ugo Rondinone was laughing, telling me about his sculpture of you at his upcoming Gladstone-Bloomberg Projects exhibition. And you, Darren? You're a nobody. That girl, Ana, she was a fling for me, a job for Downs, but you, stupid motherfucker, you actually married her. She's your fucking wife. What did you think, that you two would have a family? Move out? Get a little place out in Hackensack. Is that what you get for the money?"

Diviner breaks out into uncontrollable laughter and continues pushing Bespoke Downs' wheelchair, despite getting smacked in the head by the back of my right hand.

"The fuck you know about love, asshole."

"Actually, Darren, I think Ray here has a point. It doesn't seem like much of a marriage, with her running around with other dudes and stuff, you know? I'm not trying to sound all MAGA and shit, but you're a bit of a cuck." Downs must be trying to make me angry and it's working.

"You wanna know about love? I'll tell you about love. Love comes straight from the asshole of the devil himself. It's as pure and hot as hellfire. It wasn't until God got his meddling hands into it that things became all complicated and riddled with monogamy, jealousy, pride, flattery, vanity, and all that ugly shit. Think about it. Sexual desire is one of the few things we are hardwired to feel, along with hunger, fatigue, pissing and shitting. Tell me, is it a sin to get hungry? Do you do penance while pinching an inch every morning? So fuck all that noise. Yes, she is my wife. She is my wife because she is my soulmate. Without her I am just a rough sketch of a man. When she sees me, when I see her, we only see a masterpiece, not a rudimentary line-drawing. Even though I'm still just a defective, piece-of-shit, half-done scribble, she sees a masterful Rembrandt etching. So our love for each other creates a universe, if only for one another, where we are perfect. Well, if not perfect, then priceless."

We had stopped walking minutes ago but just now realize it.

"Fucking right," says Downs.

"Fucking A," says Diviner.

"But I don't fucking know what I'm talking about. I'm just drifting through all this shit, anyway."

"Yet here we are."

"Yes, here we are."

"Wait, where are we?"

We survey the area. The narcotics exchange has given way to a more sinister black market. The rotten smell of overripe perfume, drugs and body odor has morphed into the scent of gun bore cleaner and lubricant oil. Tables of Glocks, knives, revolvers, semi-automatics, Lugers, Woodsmen, interspersed with rolls of duct tape, zip ties, balaclavas, jars of chloroform and trihalomethane and other euphoriants make for convenient one-stop-shopping for New York's busiest night stalkers. Motorcycle gangs, Arabs, Somali, Irish Roach Boys, and Yakuza run this section of L'exchange, and they do not suffer strangers, which is not a problem for Downs and myself, who regularly spend a small fortune here. Diviner, on the other hand, is catching a few eyes. He is also known here. He would fetch a high ransom. We have to move quickly and keep our heads on a swivel. We're almost at Bedford Ave and the New Met Opera is only a half-mile from there. That half-mile though, is a gauntlet of some of the most dangerous motherfuckers on the planet, let alone in NYC.

As we pass the remaining stands of heavy weaponry, the lights flicker then go dark. Everything is black. Then a flash. A bang. Bright light. Somali pirates in a semicircle. Darkness. Light again. Bloods, Crips, gangsters gathering. I pull a knife from inside my lab coat and point my gun in all directions. Arm straight. Taking aim in between flashes of light, darkness, light, darkness. Enemies drawing closer. Fuck. I blast a round into the air. The darkness clears. Two rows of colorful Christmas lights burst into life all down the tunnel. The crowd stops encroaching. Still, I wave my gun furiously, aware of my five remaining bullets. I am the only one moving. Fuck. The crowd parts, and two men step forward from inside the menacing masses.

"Hahaha! Who the fuck are you fucking twats?" I say.

"Hey guys," says Downs. Two men, both with remarkably high cheekbones, dreamy eyes, and long braids cascading onto the padded shoulders of their oversized blazers, confront us.

"Bespoke Downs," they say in unison. "Baby, we thought you forgot our number."

"Oh," says Diviner, "you guys think you're Milli Vanilli."

"Been a long time, Bespoke," they say. "Since the orphanage."

"Hi Jerome. Hey Landry. Heard you bitches were running security for Chattergun. Driving him around and shit. I'm sure you're very proud," Bespoke smirks.

In unison they open their blazers revealing golden NYPD badges pinned to the royal blue lining of their tailored sport coats.

"New York's proudest," they say. "We've been investigating Mr. Dingman for quite some time now. Your crew has really been kicking up some shit as of late."

"The Gleaners, motherfuckers. Say the name," I sneer as everyone rolls their eyes. Fuck them.

"Let's walk, or roll, I guess. Shall we?" says Vanilli, I think.

The crowd parts and the wanna-be-pop-stars-slash-real-police escort us through the tunnel.

"We've been following you for a week now, Dingman. Knew you'd eventually head back here. Back to the New Met. We have a warrant to search your premises."

"What the fuck? A week?" Diviner interjects. "You could've, you know, stopped them from kidnapping me."

"Girl, you know that's true," Milli and Vanilli sing, "but nobody gives a shit about you, Ray. We want to talk to your girlfriend. Or is it *your* girl, Downs? Or maybe your *wife,* Darren?"

"Join the fucking club," we all say together.

"Oh, fuck off. The Gleaners ain't rats. And we certainly don't work with the fucking pigs," I say.

"So much loyalty to a woman who has betrayed you all," Milli observes.

"Not so much loyalty. More like retribution, vengeance, revenge," says Downs.

"We're almost there. But this place is totally controlled by the Resistance. I'll be hard-pressed to get Diviner and Downs through here, let alone you two freaks," I say. "Unless you wanna start a riot, I'd suggest you fill us in on your plan."

"You know all that you need to know, Darren, the grundle of the Gleaners. Do your thing. We'll be watching," the twins say.

Jerome and Landry start to sing in perfect harmony as they walk backwards into the darkness and out of sight. *Whatever you do, don't put the blame on you. Blame it on the rain, yeah yeah...*

"That was weird."

"The orphanage was a very weird place."

5

"FEAST YOUR EYES, boys, on the home of the art world's fiercest Resistance fighters, The New Met Opera." I raise my arms like a Barnum and Bailey ringleader as we step into the transfer hub at the Metropolitan Ave station. I gesture towards the stairs. "This way for the Gleaners." I point across the platform. "Over there you have the Loafing Oafs and the Scab-Exers. Down the way a bit and up the stairs you'll find Robespierre Bonnard and the Vuillard Vultures. Deeper into the G train tunnel is where David, Gena, Weiwei and the Killer River Crabs reside. We'd best keep clear of them."

Truth be told, I'm scared shitless of those ruthless bastards. David Hammons has been a wanted man ever since the snowballs he was selling showed significantly more than just trace amounts of Anthrax. Gena Rowlands has been a fugitive since that night at the Oscars when she pulled a reverse Carrie and dumped buckets of blood onto the celebrity audience, while simultaneously receiving a lifetime achievement award. Ai Weiwei, of course, has been in and out of jail for two decades. Some Chinese jails. Some Russian. Some prisons in the UK and America as well. He spent five years in a Carmen Herrera designed *Estructura Encarcelamiento* prison cell following the merger of Lisson Gallery with Core Civic, America's preeminent provider of quality corrections and detention services. All three of them are living legends. They all fill me with dread.

"Follow me," I say. "Downs, put that rifle together and

keep it ready to shoot. These groups all have spotters watching the tunnels. If you see something stir, shoot it. It may be a rat, or it may be Resistance."

"Same difference," Ray remarks.

"To get to the Gleaners, we'll have to pass the Acconci Youth. They look harmless but don't underestimate them. Stay close and let me do the talking."

Just then we all hear the thumping sound of skateboard wheels rolling against hard concrete. We hear the tail of a skateboard snap, then silence for a heartbeat, then the sound of wheels rolling faster along the platform. We look around but see nothing except flickering lights and filthy white subway tile.

"Guess the Acconci kids know we're here. Fuck, they're annoying."

We turn into the connecting tunnel with caution. It is too quiet for my liking. We stop in our tracks (in Bespoke's case quite literally). Then comes a high-pitched noise. A rising tone of guitar feedback bounces off the tile walls. The volume rises and continues rising. Impossible to tell from which direction the noise is coming from. Then another deeper, lower-toned feedback comes blaring from another indistinguishable direction. Then another. All rising in volume. I can clearly picture in my mind a Fender Tele leaning into a Twin Reverb, a Gibson 335 against a Marshall stack, a Ric against a Vox. We search around us frantically. Downs presses the scope of the sniper rifle against his eye and studiously scans the tunnels. The feedback changes to the strum of a chord. An E minor chord. In one down stroke, over and over. Oh fuck. Fuck.

"Wow, she's outdone herself," says Bespoke Downs, "a Ragnar Kjartansson performance..."

Three women emerge from the shadows wearing sparkling gold dresses and guitars slung across their shoulders, strumming E minor chords together in menacing down strokes. The echo off of the grimy white tile walls is disorienting. Behind the women in gold, a group of stray youths come into view. Dressed in baggy clothes, flannels and Chuck Taylors, with filthy long colorful hair, are the famous Resistance group known as Acconci Youth, each one with a handgun by their side. These feared performance artists gained national attention (and earned their moniker) when they live-streamed their performance of *Seedbed* from backstage at the State of the Union address. They famously commit suicide by intentional overdosing on their 28th birthdays. They are the Resistance version of spoiled brats. The Gleaners and the AY have a longstanding truce, but I still need to proceed with caution, as I'm breaking many agreements by bringing Downs and Diviner here.

"Hi, Thirsty," I say to the tall, slender girl with unwashed blonde hair who steps forward from the group. She calls herself Thirsty Moore, and for the last two years she has been the leader of the Acconci Youth. Her reign has been brutal and artless. But, for obvious reasons, the leadership of the AY changes frequently, so the Gleaners don't give a fuck.

"What's up, Dingman? Who are your friends?" She asks, even though she knows damn well who my "friends" are.

"I'm Downs. Beeeespoke Downs. Nice to meet you!"

"They're nobody," I say. "Part of a project we are working on."

"A project, eh? Funny, Ana didn't mention anything about a new project. In fact, she's been looking for Mr. Diviner. And just like that, here he is."

"Get out of the way, Thirsty, I'm bringing him to her."

The strumming of the E minor chord has changed to a muted chugging.

"Sure thing," she says but does not move.

"Hey baby," I hear behind me.

Oh fuck. It's Ana. She sounds pissed.

I recognize the tone of her voice as her "I'm being mockingly nice but you're a dead man once we're alone" voice. She smells great, like a perfect mix of body odor, cigarettes, dried sex and saliva. She claims it is her tribute to Adrian Piper but I know better. I truly love and truly fear her.

Behind her stands Jayme H. Christ and Jimmy Kanter, both giggling like children and wearing the blood-spattered-and-overly-broad-shouldered blazers once worn by Officers Milli and Vanilli.

"What's up, hoss?" Jayme says.

Josephine Bonaparte pushes her way through, looks Diviner straight in the eyes, turns to Ana and smiles, then grabs the handlebars of Bespoke Downs' wheelchair and flips him up into a wheelie. She spins him around, and they are laughing their asses off.

"Oh Josephine, my Haitian queen!" Bespoke beams. The motherfucker looks like the cat that sucked off the canary and I am filled with rage.

Jimmy Kanter walks up to Ray Diviner and guides him gently forward through the parting crowd, like an outlaw being led to the gallows.

"Let's talk, Darren. For real, baby."

Ana takes my hands and spins me around. She smiles, so lovely, and leads me to a utility closet hidden inside the tunnel walls. Inside we find one large, plush recliner and a small table lit only by a boudoir-style lamp. Ana turns and flops down on the sofa chair, so lovely. She pulls me down beside her, partially on top of her, partially on the arm of the Lazyboy. It's very awkward and very emasculating. I put my arm around her but instantly regret it. I thought it would be a high school boyfriend type power move to establish a tender dominance but that was not the case. She nestles her head into my chest and reestablishes dominance in her unique and aggressively feminine way.

"Darren, my sweet, have you ever, like, done a dramaturgical analysis of our relationship? Of our love? I mean, like, in an Erving Goffman kind of way. How would he define our current, complicated, situation?"

"We all play-act, I suppose."

Ana smiles.

"The self and the masks," she sighs.

"The staging of everyday life."

"I love you, Darren. I always have. *That* is the plot of our performance. That's the way the script was written. Yes, I am performing. I'm just saying my lines. My script says 'I love you Darren, I always have.' But if the theater is life itself, if the stage is life, then the script is the closest thing we have to a soul."

"Fuck yes. I mean, totally, but then, like, Ana, from a symbolic interactionist perspective, my defensive reflexes, or like, an instinctual form of impression management, could stimulate imaginary, yet cohesive, explanations to excuse our fucking horrible behavior in order to escape your disapproval. Which is all I've ever tried to do."

"You don't get it, baby. I was about to close the deal. But you fucked it up, D. We were about to purchase, by proxy, of course, all of the works in Diviner's show. We were about to be very rich, my love. We were planning to close the deal at the afterparty. I had buyers lined up for all of them, and I'd have had those fuckers flipped in a week. Then you stepped in. God, you're fucking stupid. Those buyers, Darren, just happen to be the same group of collectors who hired me to kill Diviner in the first place. You should know this baby, they were all early patrons of his, and they were ready to see his auction prices rise. Now, if *we* kill Diviner, while Chattergun still owns the works, well, how does *that* help us? How does *that* advance our plot?"

Ana looks at me tenderly, with wide, questioning eyes. They are so dark, so black, they swallow up time like gravity. "Oh," I say, "actually not a bad plan, baby."

Our moment was mercifully cut short by the sharp boom of a gunshot, followed by the crackle of impact against the wall tile, echoing from the adjacent tunnel. "Fuck," Ana says and jumps to her feet. We pop out of the utility closet to see Bespoke Downs pointing his rifle, with his fucking white bandana tied around his eyes, smoke pouring from the gun barrel. He is surrounded by the three E-minor strumming gold sequined women and the rag-tag Acconci Youth. Ray Diviner is duct-taped to a column about 50 yards down the platform.

"What the fuck, Downs!" I say.

"Oh, you're still here," Bespoke says nonchalantly. "A simple line painted with a brush can lead to freedom and happiness, but you know that, don't you, Dyingman? So tell me, have you begun to realize whose hand is holding that brush? I'll give you a hint. Hers is the only steady hand left."

The bastard Downs passes the rifle to my wife. She points the gun at my face, so close the heat from its barrel warms my nose and lips. My mind goes blank, then drifts into ceaselessness, into deathlessness. Unaimed memories trip over unplanned thoughts.

Over 9% of murders are committed by the last person the victim has slept with, I think, and wonder if she could singlehandedly raise that statistic solely with the men in this tunnel.

"Let him go," I say. "Diviner. Don't kill him."

I am claiming my death. Mine will be at the hands of my soulmate. Mine will be the *only* death at the hands of my soulmate, today, anyway. She will not mourn twice on the anniversary of this day.

As if a gift to me, a reward for my love, she singles me out, exclusive, unaccompanied, above my rivals. I know she is trying to tell me she loves me even though her mouth does not move. Even as her trigger-finger does.